EMERGENCY: DECEPTION

LUC

MILLS & BOON®

To Pete—
whose unconditional love
continues to give me confidence.
Pr 3:31-32

*First published in Great Britain 2003
Harlequin Mills & Boon Limited,
Eton House, 18-24 Paradise Road, Richmond, Surrey TW9 1SR*

© Lucy Clark 2003

ISBN 0 263 83450 6

*Set in Times Roman 10¼ on 11 pt.
03-0603-53168*

*Printed and bound in Spain
by Litografia Rosés, S.A., Barcelona*

CHAPTER ONE

'I REALLY appreciate your help today, Annie.' Natasha brushed her hands nervously down her navy trousers, trying to stop her hands from perspiring.

'Hey, no problem. I know what it's like, being the new girl in town.'

Natasha was surprised. 'You look so relaxed and at home here.'

The nursing sister laughed. 'Looks can be deceiving. I've only been the clinical nurse consultant for A & E for the last six months. Here we are.' She held out her hand, indicating the office door of the director of Accident and Emergency.

Natasha felt glued to the spot. She'd worked a full day in A & E but had not yet sighted the director. When she'd reported for duty that morning, his secretary had told her he would be in meetings all day and had handed her over to Annie's care.

'Nervous?' Annie asked, her short brown curls bouncing as she angled her head curiously.

Natasha shrugged and fidgeted with the pins in her bun, pushing them in tighter, making sure her hair was tidy. 'It's the *new* director. He's not the person who interviewed me for the job, or the one who hired me. What if he changes his mind?'

'It's a bit late now.' The nursing sister laughed. 'Besides, I've read your résumé. The hospital would be mad to pass you up.' Annie reached out and knocked on the door. 'I don't mind coming in and introducing you if it will make you feel any better. The new director and I knew each other when we were at school. He's an OK guy.'

Before Natasha could protest, Annie opened the door without waiting for an answer to her knock. 'Are you decent?' she called out on a laugh.

'Sure am. Come on in,' Natasha heard the deep masculine voice say. It sounded rich and smooth and vaguely…familiar. She took a deep breath to quell her uneasiness and followed the nurse in. The breath came out in a rush as she caught her first glimpse of the new A & E director.

'Brenton!' His name came out as a choked whisper and Natasha could feel her jaw drop open in complete astonishment, her eyes wide with shock.

He stared at Natasha, unable to believe she was standing before him. He broke his gaze from hers but only to quickly drink in the sight of her. She was as beautiful as his seven-and-a-half-year-old memory recalled, and he felt a tightening in his gut. Her auburn hair was pulled back into a tight, no-nonsense bun at the nape of her neck and her green eyes were vibrant with disbelief at seeing him here.

Desire began to surge again but he quickly extinguished it, remembering what she'd done to him. Remembering how she'd ripped his heart in two and discarded it without a backward glance. He clenched his jaw as she continued to openly stare at him. *'You!'*

'But…but…' Natasha's brain wasn't thinking coherently at all. Brenton was dead! How could he possibly be standing in front of her? They stared at each other for what seemed to be an eternity.

'I take it you two know each other?' Annie said into the void.

Natasha ignored the question. 'Who *are* you?' She stared into the most piercing blue eyes she'd ever seen. They were identical to the ones she'd fallen in love with all those years ago—but this man couldn't possibly be Brenton! Brenton was dead! Her heart was pounding so fast the lack of sufficient oxygen was making her feel light-headed.

He frowned. 'Who am I? What kind of question is that?' She was staring at him as though she'd seen a ghost. Her eyes were wide with confusion, with disbelief and with…fear.

Fear? She had nothing to fear from him. He might not like her very much but he would never hurt her. Ever! 'I'm Brenton. Your ex-husband. *Remember?*' His words were sarcastic but that only veiled a thread of hurt.

'No. No. You can't be.' She could feel her head starting to spin and closed her eyes for a moment.

'I think you'd better sit down,' Annie instructed, and took Natasha by the shoulders, leading her to a chair.

'No.' Natasha shrugged her off. Her breathing was coming hard and fast now and tears were blurring her vision. 'You can't be Brenton. You're not my husband.'

'*Ex*-husband,' he corrected between clenched teeth, feeling the pain and anguish he'd worked so hard to forget bubble up to the surface once more. Although he was mildly aware of his old school friend, Annie was forgotten as he stared ruthlessly at Natasha.

She shook her head, her mind still trying to cope with the solid evidence before her. She had been told, seven and a half years ago, that the man standing before her was dead. And what did he mean—*ex*-husband? She'd never divorced him! She was a widow!

'Y-you're dead.' The words were whispered but she knew he'd heard. His gaze narrowed until his eyes were small slits.

'I beg your pardon.' His voice was like steel and she recoiled as though he'd just slapped her. 'All evidence to the contrary. You left me, Tash. You upped and left me.' He slammed an angry fist onto his desk before raking a hand through his hair.

Natasha's breathing had rapidly increased and was now coming hard and fast. She sank down into the chair, her legs unable to support her any longer, her arms hanging limply at her sides. All of her energy seemed to have been sapped from her body and she felt herself get dizzy.

'Here she goes,' Annie mumbled, urging Natasha's head between her knees. Brenton watched as Annie attended Tash. The nurse raised her head to look at him. It was her don't-argue-with-me look and the tone of her voice as she spoke added force to it. 'Take it easy on her, Monty.'

'Monty?' Natasha jerked her head up and looked from Brenton to the nurse and back again. His gaze met hers and she saw disgust and…hatred in his eyes. *Hatred?* Why? No! This man was definitely not her husband. 'Your name is Monty?'

'Where did I supposedly die?' He ignored her question, wanting to get some answers to her ridiculous statement. Dead! Of course he wasn't dead. He was standing right in front of her.

She closed her eyes, trying to compute the question, trying to think.

'Where?'

'In South America.'

'When?'

'It will be eight years on July the fifth.'

'Who told you I was dead?'

'You're *not* Brenton.'

'Who told you?' he reiterated. She knew that tone of his. It was the one where people had pushed him too far—and he'd never used it with her. Until now.

Something was drastically wrong with this picture. She knew it, she felt it, but she had no idea what it was. How could Brenton possibly think she'd leave him? He clenched his jaw and crossed his arms impatiently then raised an eyebrow—she'd always loved the way he did that—indicating he was still waiting for her answer. The familiarity, the scent of him—both came flooding back. It helped her to find some strength and as she continued to hold his gaze, she lifted her chin defiantly. 'Who? Who told me you were dead? Why, your mother, of course. Who else?'

That shocked him and he stared at her with incredulity. 'My *mother?*' He shook his head in disbelief. 'My *mother* told you I was dead.'

'Yes.'

'No. You're lying.'

'I'm not.'

He shook his head again. 'Stubborn as ever. Where?'

'Sorry?'

'Where were you when she told you this…news?'

'She came to our apartment.'

He smiled mercilessly. 'Now I know you're lying. My mother hated that apartment and vowed when we moved in that she'd never set foot in it.'

'Well, she did.' Natasha wanted to prove him wrong. 'She came to tell me that you'd died. Then she took me to the hospital.'

'Why?'

He still didn't believe her. Whoever this man was, he didn't believe a single word she was saying. The pounding in Natasha's head started to increase and she closed her eyes.

'Why?' he asked again.

She opened her eyes and looked directly at him. 'Because I passed out.'

'But you never faint.' The statement was made with solid conviction.

Tears were welling up in Natasha's eyes and there wasn't much she could do to stop them flowing over. If this man was indeed Brenton, then she should be happy, not feeling as though her world had come to an end.

When he saw the tears gathering in her eyes, he felt awful. He'd made Tash cry. The instant he felt the emotion, he squashed it, telling himself firmly that she deserved it. She'd pulled the wool over his eyes. She'd lied and cheated and he was determined never to let her get the upper hand again.

Natasha wiped at the tears with trembling hands as she met his gaze. It was as hard as granite but the message she saw there was clear. This isn't over, it said, and she completely agreed. Finally, she turned to look at Annie.

'Feel like standing up?' Annie's softness was like a lifeline.

'Yes, I think I can try,' she replied after a moment's hesitation, and allowed Annie to help her up. She squared her shoulders and tilted her chin, hoping she looked braver than she felt.

'Welcome to Geelong General Hospital.' Brenton's tone was emotionless as he held out a folder. 'Here is a list of your duties. If you have any questions, make an appointment with my secretary.' He nodded and sat down in his chair, returning his focus to his work, ignoring her completely.

On wooden legs, Natasha turned and walked out of there—heading back to the female change rooms to collect her bag. She punched her identification number into the locker she'd been assigned that morning. Morning—it seemed like a lifetime ago.

Her legs started to tremble and she slumped down onto a bench positioned between the banks of lockers. It was then she realised her entire body was trembling.

'Well, you've certainly had a lot of excitement for your first day at work,' Annie remarked as she walked into the change rooms. The nurse sat beside her and smiled encouragingly.

'Who was that man?'

'Monty?'

'So his name *isn't* Brenton?' Natasha clutched the hope that she wasn't going completely insane.

'Yes, it is. Monty's a nickname. His middle name, really.'

Natasha gasped. 'You *know* about that?'

'Sure. Anyone who went to school with him does. Brenton James Montague Worthington the third. Hey, are you feeling all right? You're starting to look a little shaky again.'

Natasha couldn't get rid of the permanent lump in her throat. 'I'm fine,' she said absent-mindedly. 'It's really him.' The tears started to trickle down her cheeks. 'I was told he was dead.' She searched in her pocket for a tissue and, when she found one, blew her nose. 'He doesn't believe me.'

'He's had a shock himself,' Annie defended him. 'Give it some time.'

Natasha laughed ironically and shook her head. 'That's what the psychologist said to me in the years of therapy I had after I was told my husband had died. ''Give it time,'' he'd say. ''Time heals all wounds.'' Well, it doesn't.'

'No,' Annie agreed. 'But time does help us to accept and move on.'

'And what happens to the ''moving on'' process when you discover you've been lied to? When the past seven and a half years of my life—*our* lives have been stolen from us? How are we supposed to accept and move on?'

Annie shrugged. 'I have no idea.'

Brenton threw his pen down in disgust when the two women left his office. Closing his eyes, he massaged his temples, trying to get rid of the headache he could feel coming on. Thank goodness it was the end of the day and he didn't need to deal with seeing her again until tomorrow—at least he now had time to prepare himself.

What were the odds? He shook his head in disbelief. Natasha was here. Natasha…what? What was her surname? He hunted through the mounds of paperwork he'd inherited from his predecessor until he found the right file. He flicked it open. '''Natasha Forest,''' he read out loud. 'Forest?' It wasn't her maiden name so why was she now Natasha Forest? After they'd married, she'd said she wanted to practise under her married name of Natasha Worthington. Obviously she hadn't been that attached to it.

Perhaps she'd married the father of her child. The headache pounded even more at the thought but then he recalled that she hadn't been wearing a wedding ring. He knew because his gaze had slid over those long slender fingers and her left hand had been bare.

Her right hand hadn't.

His gut tightened in exactly the same way it had when he'd first noticed the ring. It was a white gold band with small inset diamonds placed in a decorative pattern all the way around. He knew the ring well. He should because he'd chosen it and given it to her on their wedding day.

If she'd married someone else, why did she still wear it?

He shook his head again, trying to clear it from the continuous flow of questions. What about her child? He knew she'd been pregnant—at least, that's what his mother had told him when he'd returned from South America to find his wife gone. Pregnant by another man. Was the child responsible for the dark circles he'd noticed beneath her eyes? No. Come to think of it, he didn't want to know. The past had been hard enough to get through. He didn't want to go there again.

He shook his head and raked a hand through his hair. She'd lost a lot of weight—not that she'd been overweight before but she certainly hadn't been skin and bone as she was now. There was no denying her beauty. Her auburn hair and green eyes were a potent mixture. The tightening in his gut increased and he clenched his jaw.

Now she was here—at Geelong General Hospital. His hospital. She would be working closely with him for the next six months!

So what?

She was his ex-wife.

So what?

She was going to be working closely with him.

So what?

She'd ripped his heart out and discarded it.

So what?

He was a professional and he would stay in control of his emotions.

Natasha wiped her eyes and stood. 'Sorry, Annie. I've kept you long enough.'

'It's fine,' Annie told her. 'I've just got a bit of paperwork to catch up on before I leave tonight. Nothing urgent.'

The door to the change rooms burst open. 'Annie?'

'Yes?'

'I've been beeping you,' one of the nurses said as she walked in. Natasha turned away, not wanting the nurse to see her red-rimmed eyes.

'Sorry.' Annie glanced down at her pager. 'Battery's dead. Problem?'

'You're needed.'

'OK. I'll be right there,' she said dismissively. Natasha could feel the nurse's curiosity before the woman walked out, leaving her alone with Annie again. 'What was I just saying about my workload?' Annie groaned. 'Ah…A & E—boring one minute, hectic the next.'

Natasha dredged up a smile and looked at her new friend. 'Hope it's nothing too bad.'

'I'll cope. You go on home.' Annie peered at her closely. 'Will you be all right to drive?'

'Should be. It's not far but I promise to clear my head while I'm on the road.'

'You'd better,' Annie said as she headed to the door. 'See you tomorrow.'

Natasha sat down again and shook her head. It was impossible. Everything was impossible. How was she supposed to work here for the next six months? How were *they* supposed to work together? He hated her!

Tears started to well in her eyes again but she brushed them away impatiently. 'No. You're going to calm down until you get home. *Then* you can fall in a heap,' she said out loud. She splashed some water on her face before adding a fresh coat of lipstick and slipping her sunglasses on. Picking up her briefcase, she pulled out her car keys, squared her shoulders and headed for the door.

She wouldn't give him another thought, she told herself as she walked down the corridor and past his office. The door was shut. She clamped her teeth on her tongue as her breathing started to increase.

She wouldn't think about it at all, she decided as she headed through the car park, willing the tears away.

She would remain poised and in control, she told herself as her trembling hand fumbled with the keys. She put her briefcase down and brushed her hand impatiently beneath her

sunglasses, wiping her eyes so she could focus better. Finally
the key went into the lock and she opened the door.

She wouldn't succumb to these overpowering feelings, she
told herself sternly as she inserted the ignition key. Not just
yet…but her emotions were too powerful for her brain to
control. Natasha slumped forward onto the steering-wheel and
began to cry.

Brenton felt the lump in his own throat constrict at the sight
of her. He'd been unlocking his own car, parked two rows
back from Natasha's, when he'd noticed her striding purposefully in his direction. At first he'd thought she'd been on her
way to talk to him but then she'd stopped by a car and had
taken her time unlocking it.

It was then he'd realised she was upset.

His first instinct had been to rush to her, to take her in his
arms and hold her while she cried. Then reality had kicked
in. He had no idea why she was crying and perhaps it was
all an act. Perhaps she'd seen him and had decided to twist
his guts into an even tighter knot by pretending to cry. After
all, she'd pretended throughout their marriage that she'd loved
him so anything was possible.

Clenching his teeth together, his headache increased. He
needed to get home. He needed to think. Climbing into his
car, he started the engine and reversed out of the space. He
needed to come up with some sort of plan to help get him
through the next six months because right now he was positive his heart was not going to survive if he didn't.

The sound of another car leaving the car park startled
Natasha and she lifted her head. Taking off her sunglasses
she searched through her briefcase for a tissue. After wiping
her eyes and blowing her nose, she took a deep, shaky breath.

It's not far to drive, so just concentrate on the road and
don't think about him, she told herself sternly. She managed
it, but only just.

She climbed from her car and let herself into her aunt's big
rambling house, dumping her keys and briefcase by the back
door. She headed up the passage, hoping to make it safely to

her room without being caught. Somehow she managed it. Collapsing onto the bed, she gave way to the tears.

'Mummy?'

Natasha jerked upright and quickly wiped her eyes. 'Hey, honey.' Lily was standing at the base of her bed. 'I didn't hear you.' She held out her hand to Lily and the six-year-old girl climbed onto the bed.

'Mummy, what's wrong?'

Natasha sighed as she gave Lily a big hug. 'I've just had a busy day but now that I'm here with you, I'm feeling much better.' It was true. 'I missed you today, Lil.'

'Yeah. I missed you too, Mum.' Lily gave her mother a kiss and Natasha felt more tension seep out of her.

'How was your first day at your new school?'

'Uh, you know.' Lily shrugged.

'Did anyone play with you at lunchtime?'

'Yeah, this girl called Rachael, but that was for recess. At lunchtime, I played with Matthew.'

'That's good. And is your teacher nice?'

'Oh, yeah, she's the coolest, and guess what, Mum.'

Natasha smiled, knowing there was no need to reply as Lily would just continue on in her usual effervescent way.

'The class has a classroom-manager and Rachael picked me. I'm going to be the classroom-manager tomorrow and I get to help Miss Schlowski put the day of the week up and what the weather is like and I get to call out the roll with the kids' names on and if there are any jobs that need doing then I get to do them but someone has to come with me because we're too young to walk around the school by ourselves but that's all right because I'm not really sure where I'm going and then at the end of the day I get to pick someone else to be classroom-manager and I think I'll pick Matthew because he played with me at lunchtime.'

Natasha laughed. This was just what she needed. A dose of Lily. She hugged her daughter close. 'I'm so glad you had a good first day, sweetheart.'

'Dinner!' Aunt Jude called through the house.

'Come on. We'd better not keep Aunt Jude waiting.'

'Wash your hands,' Aunt Jude called, and Natasha smiled feeling a lot braver than she had half an hour ago.

So what?

She'd had a big shock.

So what?

She would have to work with Brenton.

So what?

She had to work harder to control her emotions.

So what?

Brenton was alive…and he hated her!

CHAPTER TWO

NATASHA pushed the thought from her mind, determined to enjoy her family. For so long it had just been Lily and herself. Oh, sure, they'd had great friends who'd always supported them, but when Aunt Jude had decided she'd had enough of trotting the globe and was going to settle in Geelong, Natasha had known the time had been right for a move.

She owed Aunt Jude a lot—respect being top of the list. Her father's sister, Aunt Jude was the only person who had really cared about her—family-wise. Now Natasha had someone to look after Lily while she was working and also didn't have to worry about cleaning and maintaining a house. Not having to cook meals was a definite bonus and as Aunt Jude loved doing it, who was she to argue?

'Well, hurry it up,' Aunt Jude gently chastised. 'The meal will be as cold as ice with the way you two are dawdling, and I didn't go to all this trouble to eat cold food.'

Natasha kissed her aunt's cheek. 'Thank you. It looks and smells marvellous. You're wonderful.'

'Oh, get away with you.' Aunt Jude said, slightly embarrassed.

'No, I won't,' Natasha said as she sat down. 'You've been under-appreciated for years and Lily and I are determined to make it up to you. Aren't we, Lil?'

'Yep.'

'So you may was well just say thank you and learn how to accept the compliment.'

'Thank you,' Aunt Jude said placatingly, but couldn't keep the smile from her face.

After dinner, Natasha checked Lily's homework and listened to her read before tucking her up in bed. 'Straight to

17

sleep tonight,' she instructed. 'You're a little bit later than usual.'

'That's because Aunt Jude wanted to wait for you so we could all have dinner together after your first day at work.'

'It *was* nice but now…' Natasha waggled a finger at her daughter. 'Straight to sleep.' She kissed her daughter once more before leaving the room. She got changed and went in search of her aunt. They had much to discuss.

Three cups of tea and almost a whole box of tissues later, Aunt Jude shook her head in disbelief.

'He's alive?'

'Yes.'

'And you're absolutely sure it's him?'

'Sure.' Natasha nodded and blew her nose again.

'How? I mean…' Aunt Jude shook her head.

'I know. Ever since I saw him, my head has been spinning with questions. What happened? Where has he been all these years? What about Lily? How on earth do I tell him about Lily? Why didn't he look for me?' Natasha's voice cracked and she buried her head in the lounge cushions. 'I feel as though I've been put through the wringer. Every bone in my body aches and these…' She sat up again and pointed to her eyes. 'I feel as though I've sprung a leak. I can't stop crying.'

'Well, you have good reason to cry.'

'I know but…' Natasha bit her lip. 'He looked at me as though he hates me. How? How could Brenton possibly hate me? I didn't do anything to him. *I'm* the one who's had to pick up the pieces of my life and get on with things, and it wasn't easy. It still isn't.'

'His mother told you he was dead, didn't she?' Aunt Jude asked rhetorically.

'Yes.' Natasha leaned her weary body back against the cushions. 'She came to our apartment.'

'That poky little place you'd rented.'

'That's the one. Brenton and I wanted to do it on our own without any help from his trust fund.'

'I thought his mother cut him off without a cent when he married you.'

'So did I, but he told me that the regular sum of money was still deposited into his account throughout the six months of our marriage.'

'Did either of you use it?'

'No…at least, not that I know of. We were focusing on saving the deposit for our house.'

'And Brenton never suggested using that money?'

'No. He was as determined as I was to support ourselves. We'd planned on looking around at houses once Brenton got back from South America.' Natasha trailed off as a fresh bout of tears started to form in her eyes. 'I've just been thinking of everything we lost. Seven and a half years!'

'Why would his mother do that? Tell you he was dead when he wasn't?'

Natasha shook her head. 'I don't know. Control?'

'Well, she's obviously lied to you, which means…'

'She's lied to Brenton.' The fog started clearing a little from Natasha's brain. 'He looks at me as though he hates me, Aunt Jude.'

'His mother never did like you.'

Natasha's mobile phone started ringing and she raced out into the hall where she'd dumped her briefcase, hoping to stop the noise before it woke Lily.

'Dr Forest.' There was silence on the other end of the line. 'Hello?'

'We need to talk.' There was no mistaking Brenton's voice.

Natasha started trembling all over again. She felt warmth course through her at his deep tone yet she also detected anger and hurt. Forcing herself to take a breath, she gasped and then coughed. 'Yes,' she spluttered. 'Yes, we do.'

'Are you free now?'

'Now?' Natasha checked her watch. Half past nine. 'Uh…what did you have in mind? I mean, did you want to meet somewhere? That might be a bit difficult for me.'

'Because of your child?'

Natasha's back straightened at his self-righteous tone. 'H-how do you know about her?'

'Your résumé. Next to marital status it says "Widowed, one child,"' he replied impatiently.

'Oh.' Well, he could hate her all he liked but she wasn't going to let him think of Lily in any light other than favourable. 'She's one of the reasons, yes.'

He was silent again but she let the silence hang. After all, *he'd* called *her.*

'What's your address?'

'You're coming here?' she blurted, and quickly lowered her voice. 'You want to come here? Now?'

'Look, Tash, we need to talk and I think it's better if we do it before our duty shift tomorrow.'

He had a point. 'All right.' She gave him her address and he instantly hung up. No goodbye, no 'see you soon'. She walked back into the lounge room where Aunt Jude was sitting in front of the air-vent, trying to get cool in the hot February weather. Even though the sun had gone down, it was still quite warm. 'He's coming around.'

'What? Now?'

'Yes.'

Aunt Jude scanned the room and quickly started picking things up and putting them away. She pounded some cushions and set them perfectly in place. 'Well, don't just stand there, girl, go and put some water on that blotchy face of yours.'

'Good idea.' Natasha headed for the bathroom. Ten minutes later, she was dressed more presentably in a pair of shorts and a summer top rather than her baggy house clothes. Why she was making the effort, she wasn't quite sure. Was it for herself or Brenton? After all, he'd seen her dressed in her baggy house clothes a hundred times before but she didn't feel comfortable opening the door dressed like a slob, especially as she'd had prior warning of his visit.

When a knock at the door finally came, she froze, overwhelmed with apprehension. At least he hadn't rung the door bell. It was a guaranteed way to wake Lily up quickly and right now she preferred her daughter to remain sound asleep.

She opened the door, realising her hands were shaking and her mouth had gone dry. Her heart rate accelerated at the sight of him. He was everything she remembered, except for the scowl.

They stood staring at each other for a few minutes. He was still dressed in his work clothes, although his shirtsleeves were rolled up to his elbows, his tie had been removed and he'd untucked his shirt, the way he always did at the end of the day. Natasha shook her head, annoyed that she remembered the most intimate details about this man.

'May I come in or should we talk in the doorway?' he drawled, his scowl disappearing for a fraction of a second.

'Oh…Sorry.' She unlocked the screen door. 'Come through.' She stepped back and waited for him to pass. He pulled the screen door closed quickly behind him, ensuring no flies came into the house. He smelled subtly of sweat but also anti-perspirant. He hadn't changed that either and every time she'd smelt that same scent she'd associated it with Brenton.

She led the way into the lounge room. 'We can talk in here.'

He walked in and looked around the room at the books on the shelves as well as the videos by the television. 'Comfortable room.'

'Yes.' What was he looking for?

'Not many photographs. You used to love having photographs lining the walls.'

'Well, this is Aunt Jude's home. We've only been in Geelong for two weeks and most of that has been filled with unpacking and shopping, although there are still many boxes to go.'

'Hmm.' The scowl was back.

'Can I get you a drink?'

'Iced water would be great, thanks.'

She smiled as the memory returned. When Brenton drank

cold drinks, he liked them icy cold. 'I won't be a moment.' She hurried from the room and into the kitchen. There, she leaned against the bench and took five very deep breaths, hoping in vain that it might actually control the wild tattoo rhythm of her heart.

She returned with two glasses of iced water and placed them on the coffee-table.

'I'll come right to the point,' he stated as he sat down opposite her. 'Today was a shock to the system.'

'You can say that again.' Natasha nodded slowly.

Brenton stared at her for a moment. 'Did you really believe I was dead?'

A lump formed in her throat and she nodded again, pursing her lips together in an effort to control her emotions. 'Ever since the fifth of July, seven and a half years ago.'

'Did you grieve for me?'

'Of course I did. What kind of question is that?' she retorted hotly.

He stood up and looked down at her accusingly. 'Why is your surname Forest?'

Natasha held his gaze, lifting her chin with a hint of defiance. 'When you said you wanted to come and talk, Brenton, I hadn't expected to be cross-examined.'

'Why is your surname Forest?' he repeated.

'Because I remarried.'

He shoved his hands into his pockets. 'So you *really* grieved for me, eh?'

She stood. 'That's enough.'

'It's not enough,' he retorted, and she shushed him.

'Keep your voice down. You can be cross with me all you like but I won't have you waking my daughter.'

He raised an eyebrow in acknowledgement and started pacing the room. 'When did you remarry?'

'Three and a half years ago.'

'What about the guy you ran off with?'

'What guy?' Her tone was defensive.

'The guy you left me for.'

'I didn't *leave* you.'

'I beg to differ. When I returned from South America, you were gone.'

'I was told you were dead.' She said the words clearly and with determination.

He stalked over to stand in front of her. 'By my mother.'

'Yes.' She willed her body not to respond to his nearness, the way his scent was washing over her senses.

'At our apartment.' His hands tightened into fists as he breathed in the distracting perfume she wore. Her hair was at her shoulders and it was all he could do to hang onto his anger and not sift his hands through the auburn locks.

'Yes.' She continued to hold his gaze.

'Where were you living?'

'Wangaratta.'

'Wangaratta,' he repeated, and forced himself to take a step away before he dragged her into his arms and took her mouth fiercely with his. He ground his teeth together and turned his back to her. He shook his head and when he turned back, there was pain and hurt reflected deeply in his eyes. 'How could you, Tash? How could you marry another man?'

'You were dead.'

'How did you know? Did you see my dead body?'

'No but your mother showed me your ashes. She said it was easier to get you cremated in South America—more efficient and less morbid. Those were her exact words, Brenton. You were dead. She gave me the death certificate and as you're standing in front of me today, it was obviously forged.'

'How could my mother possibly get a forged South American death certificate?' he asked incredulously.

'How should I know? Money? Power? Corruption?'

'But why?'

'Isn't it obvious? She wanted us apart—for good.'

'She certainly went to a lot of trouble.'

'Well, it worked, didn't it?'

'What about this man…Forest? Where is he now?'

'He's dead.'

'Can you be sure of that?' There was a hint of disbelief in his tone and Natasha glared at him, her eyes blazing with anger.

'Yes, I can, because I was working at the hospital when they brought him into A & E.' She impatiently brushed hot tears from her eyes. 'Conrad had been driving home from a friend's place and had a car accident. He died in surgery. That was over three years ago. We had just under six months together.'

If she'd wanted him to feel bad, she'd succeeded, and it diffused his anger like air rushing out of a balloon. 'I'm sorry,' he stated when she finally looked at him. 'It must have been a horrible time for you.'

Natasha sighed heavily, pushing the hair away from her face. 'There's so much between us, Brenton, and I don't know if I have the strength to wade through it all. There's already been so much pain.'

He crossed his arms across his chest. 'We have to, Tash.'

'But at what cost?'

He shrugged. 'Whatever it takes. Since I arrived this evening, we've already moved past the awkwardness of being in the same room as each other. We need to unravel this web, Tash.'

Her bottom lip started to quiver in response to his softened tone. 'You have no idea what I've been through, Brenton— just as I have no idea what's happened to you.'

'Do you want to know?'

'Yes and no.'

'At least you're being honest about it.'

'I'm an honest person. In that respect, I *know* I haven't changed.'

'Really?' His tone was sceptical.

'What's that supposed to mean?'

He shook his head and raked a hand through his hair. 'I don't understand how you could have thought I was dead. I was overseas for two months, Tash. That's all. Eight weeks!'

'And it was at the end of the fifth week that your mother came to our apartment and told me the news.'

'Why would she come to the apartment? That's what doesn't make any sense. Why didn't you summon you to her home, like she always had? She never came to the apartment, Tash. She hated that place.'

'Only because it spoke of your independence from her.' She shrugged. 'I don't know why she didn't ask me to come to her home. Perhaps she felt Toorak wasn't the place to break the news that my husband had died. Perhaps she thought I might throw up on her Persian carpets. I don't know, B.J.'

He couldn't help the thread of pleasure which shot through him at her absent-mindedly calling him B.J. It was a nickname only Natasha used and one he found he still liked hearing from her lips.

'But she *did* come to the apartment and I knew the instant I saw her there that, whatever she had to say, it wasn't going to be pleasant.' Natasha smiled to herself. 'Perhaps it was just as well she came to the apartment because I *did* throw up, narrowly missing her designer shoes, before passing out.'

Brenton frowned as though it didn't make sense. 'You're not prone to fainting.'

'No.'

'Had you ever fainted before?'

'No.'

'Since?'

'No.'

'Not even when your…other husband died?'

'No. I did, however, work myself into a near nervous breakdown, denying the emotions of having not one but *two* husbands die—before I was twenty-eight. I felt jinxed!' She looked down at the floor before returning to meeting his gaze. 'Until today.'

He saw the pain in her eyes intensify. It wasn't right for a woman as beautiful as she was to have been through so much. *If*, he reminded himself, *if* what she was saying was the truth.

She took a few steps towards him. 'Today I found out I've

only been widowed once.' Her words were a whisper but they wound themselves around him. She came to stand before him and slowly raised her hand to push his already ruffled hair back into place. He closed his eyes, savouring the feel of her fingers combing through his hair while fighting the urge to do likewise to her.

He clenched his jaw and opened his eyes, trying to control his heartbeat. Her eyes were closed and her lips were slightly parted, and it took superhuman strength for him to resist. His hand circled her wrist and her eyes snapped open.

The way she was gazing up at him made him want to forget everything. The past and the future were inconsequential when she looked at him with those desire-filled green eyes. It had always been that way. Ever since their first kiss, he'd been completely captivated by her.

Acknowledging the power she held over him was enough to help him step away.

'B.J.?' Her voice was soft, confused but he let her hand go. He heard the regret in her tone and desperately tried to harden his heart against it. She'd left him, he reminded himself. When he'd returned from South America, she had been gone.

He turned away. 'You said my mother gave you a death certificate.'

'Yes.'

'May I see it?'

Natasha thought for a moment, trying to remember where it might be. Her hesitation caused him to turn and look at her with fresh doubt. 'It's still in one of the boxes which needs unpacking but I will definitely find it for you.'

'I'd appreciate it.' He eyed her cautiously for a long moment before looking away. 'I'd better go.'

'No.' She took a step towards him. 'Wait. There's something else we need to talk about.'

'What?'

'My daughter.'

'What about her?'

'Well…um…' She motioned to the lounge. 'Do you want to sit down?'

'No.'

'OK. Well…ah…Lily is…' Oh, gosh. How did she say this? How was she supposed to tell him that Lily was his daughter.

'Lily?'

She decided that actions would speak louder than words. 'Come with me.'

'Where—?'

'Shh. Quietly,' she whispered. She walked up the hallway and stopped by a door that was slightly ajar, a small night-light shining out into the darkened room. 'Come and have a look.'

Brenton didn't want to go. He didn't want to look at the child she'd had with some other man, but curiosity got the better of him and he found himself following her into the room. He stared at the bed which was in the corner of the room, at a desk with a computer against the far wall and colourful pictures on the walls. Little-girl pictures of dolls and teddy bears. On the wall above her bed hung an embroidered name banner with 'Lily' carefully stitched on it.

The child in the bed was sprawled out beneath the thin cotton sheet. Her hair was the same colour as her mother's, or perhaps a bit lighter, but where Natasha's was almost straight, this little girl had an abundance of curls which seemed to be tied up on top of her head.

His mother had told him Natasha had been having an affair the instant he'd left for South America. Was this true? Was this child from that affair? If what Natasha was saying was true…then he couldn't take anything his mother had said as gospel any more.

Another thought entered his head and he looked from Natasha to the sleeping child and back again. She was called Lily. A name he loved. Could this little girl be…? No. He stopped his thoughts there and quickly turned and left the room.

He knew Natasha was right behind him because his body was aware of her presence. It had always been that way and today, he'd discovered, nothing had changed.

'Brenton.' Even the way she said his name, almost like a caress, hadn't changed. They returned to the lounge room and he started to prowl around like a caged panther. He stopped on the other side of the room and pointed a finger towards the door. 'You can't expect me to believe that…that…'

'Yes.' She nodded. 'I can. Brenton…Lily is *your* daughter. You're her father.'

CHAPTER THREE

NATASHA had never seen Brenton so stunned in her life. He allowed Natasha to lead him to a chair before slumping down into it, staring unseeingly at the wall in front of him. Natasha sat down beside him and waited. She wasn't sure what to do. Should she say something? Should she leave him alone for a while? Should she hold his hand?

Eventually, he spoke. 'Are…are you sure?'

It was a fair question…but it hurt. It hurt so much that he would doubt her word. 'Yes.' She took a deep breath. 'But…um…if you wanted to have a test done, I understand.' Natasha cleared over the lump in her throat and clenched her hands tightly together.

'When?'

Tears gathered in her eyes. He *really* didn't believe her! Even though a blood test would give him the result he needed, she was reluctant to put Lily through it. 'Well, I could organise for her to be tested—'

'I'm not talking about a test, Tash, I'm asking when was she conceived. How old is she?'

'She's six. Well, she'll be seven in March.' She smiled slightly and her tone was wistful with memories. 'It was the last night we spent together before you left for South America.'

'But you were on the Pill.'

'And you, as a doctor, should realise that the Pill isn't one hundred per cent effective. I was stunned when I found out.'

'Why didn't you tell me?'

'I didn't have the chance.' Her words were a whisper and she took a deep breath, trying to gather the strength to remember *that* day. She shifted on the lounge cushions so she was facing him. 'I had been feeling a little off colour ever since you'd left, but I just put it down to the fact that I was missing you.' Her lower lip started to tremble and one of the tears that had been balancing on her eyelashes spilled over and rolled down her cheek.

'I know it's hard, Tash.' His gentle tone was almost her undoing. He reached out and tenderly brushed her tear away. The brief touch had her heart racing out of control. 'But I *need* to know.'

She nodded and swallowed. As hard as it might be, she owed him the truth. He was the man she had loved with all her heart…and her best friend. 'I was chatting with one of your intern friends to see if anyone else had had stomach flu and she told me there wasn't any stomach flu going around. She asked me when my last cycle was and it was only then that I stopped and counted up the weeks. We went to the hospital pharmacy, got a test and did it straight away. It was positive.' She smiled at him. 'I'd never been happier, or prouder, Brenton, to think I was carrying our child. I was going to call you that night, but when I arrived home your mother was there, waiting for me. My stomach twisted in knots when I saw her black limo sitting outside the front of our apartment block.

'When I asked her what she wanted, she said we would talk inside. *That* surprised me, knowing how she hated the place, but we went inside. She had an expression on her face as though she'd just stepped in something disgusting. She perched herself on the chair and said she had some bad news.' Natasha looked away, her vision blurring because of the tears she was trying to hold back. Her lower lip was trembling and she bit it, forcing herself to go on.

'She even had tears in her eyes, Brenton. She dabbed at them with a lace handkerchief and then told me she'd received a phone call from the aid organisation who'd sent you to South America in the first place, informing her of your death. She said they'd been trying to call me all day and when they'd received no answer, they'd called her instead. Then she broke down and cried. *Really* cried.'

'*My* mother?' He was back to disbelieving her. 'My mother never cried—never! Even when my father died—nothing.'

'Nothing that *you* saw. How can you possibly say she never cried? How could you know that?'

'Hmm,' was all he said, his frown speaking volumes. 'So what did you do?'

'I was just too stunned at first. I couldn't believe what she was telling me. Slowly as it sank in, I started to feel weak. My head started spinning and I couldn't seem to focus.' More tears rolled down her cheeks and he tenderly brushed them away again. 'That's all I remember. The next time I opened my eyes, I was in hospital. Not our hospital but a private one. The nurse said I'd been out for about an hour, which I thought was kind of a long time, but she said when suffering from severe emotional trauma, it's quite common. They kept me in for a few weeks, worried I might miscarry.

'Your mother came to see me the following day. She said the best thing I could do with my life now was to move on. She made it clear that as I had no family here, it would be best for me to get right away from Melbourne and the people who would remind me of you.'

'But what about med school?'

'That's what I said, and she told me she had arranged for me to finish it via correspondence and to do my internship at another hospital away from the city. I found out later that she'd made a sizable donation to the hospital where I did my internship but at the time I was too distraught with grief to care. I let her make the plans, I let her take over because…' Natasha choked on a sob. 'Because…' She took a few deep breaths, trying to find the courage to say the words. 'Because you were gone and all I wanted to do was to go with you. I wanted to die, too.'

She couldn't hold the flood at bay any longer and broke down, sobbing. Without another thought, Brenton gathered her into his arms, holding her tightly. The feel of her pressed up against him once more was as agonising as it was sweet. He'd missed her, he realised. Even though she'd caused him so much pain, he'd still missed her, and the knowledge shocked him. He breathed in her perfume and closed his eyes with longing. She fitted perfectly into his arms. Would she fit as perfectly into his life?

As wave after wave of unhappiness came over her, Brenton's desire to protect her from any further hurt became overwhelming. He'd taken a vow to love, honour and cherish this woman, and it was a feeling too powerful to fight.

Natasha cried as she had all those years ago. Cried for the web of lies which had been woven about them and cried for the time they'd missed. Throughout it all Brenton held her, murmuring soothing words and stroking her back.

The feel of him, his firm chest beneath her cheek, the scent of him and the way his hand was wreaking havoc with her equilibrium did nothing to sooth her wayward emotions. She wanted to stay here for ever, secure in the embrace of his arms, but she knew she couldn't.

'You smell so good.' The words were out before he could stop them. He buried his face in the hair at her neck and nuzzled, groaning with pleasure. 'You're so much…you, Tash. It's driving me crazy.'

'Is that a bad thing?' she whispered near his ear, her body flooded with tingles from both his words and the feel of his breath hot on her neck.

With superhuman effort, Brenton eased away from her, staring down into her red-rimmed eyes. She was beautiful. It was a fact, pure and simple. They stared at each other for a few long moments, neither of them able to move.

All Natasha wanted right this second was for him to press his lips to hers and tell her that everything was going to be all right, but she knew he would never utter those words unless he believed them to be absolutely true. Life just wasn't that simple.

Finding the strength from somewhere, he looked away and stood up. The moment passed.

'I'm sorry,' she whispered. 'It's just so…hard.'

'Don't apologise.' His voice was thick with emotion. He cleared his throat. 'I take it my mother didn't know about the baby?'

Natasha shook her head. 'She never said anything about it but she must have realised as that was the main reason they kept me in hospital for so long.'

'Did she visit you after that first day?'

'A few times, but it was brief and to the point each time. She brought your cremated ashes to the church chapel and we had a little service for you.'

'Just the two of you?'

'Yes, and the chaplain. She said she wanted it to be private and didn't want the media attention.'

'And this was all right with you?'

Natasha raised her eyebrows at his accusatory tone. 'All I knew was that you were dead. I didn't care about anything else.'

'Did she get you to sign any papers?'

'Yes. She wanted me to sign forms from the university saying I agreed to complete med school via correspondence— things like that. I know there was a document which she made me sign to waive any claim to the Worthington fortune.'

He scowled and she wasn't sure whether it was for her— or his mother. 'And did you?'

'Yes.'

'But what about the baby?'

'All I knew was that I wanted your mother to have nothing to do with her grandchild and if signing that document ensured her distance, then I would gladly take it. So I did. She wanted me out of your life, Brenton, and she made that abundantly clear when I left Melbourne. She gave me quite a substantial amount of money, saying it was for relocation costs, and added that she never wanted to see me again. She said it was fortuitous in a way that you had died because our lives together would have been fraught with pain and misery. At least this way your death had provided a clean break and I *had* to move on.'

'She said *what?* No. I know she was manipulative but surely she wouldn't say such things like that.'

'It's the truth, Brenton. I would never lie to you.' He glanced away as she said the words and Natasha was left with the feeling that he didn't quite believe her. 'I slapped her face.'

'What?'

'When she said that to me, I slapped her across the face. I was so consumed with rage that she could possibly think your death was the best solution to our life together that I had no words—none—to adequately convey how distraught I was.'

'You *slapped* my *mother!*' He stared at her, his jaw hanging open in shock.

'Yes.' Natasha straightened her shoulders, unsure why she felt the need to defend her actions.

'You know she died?'

'I'd heard. Two years ago, wasn't it?'

'Yes. We were having lunch and she suffered a massive heart attack. Nothing I did made any difference.'

Natasha stood and reached out her hand to him but he avoided her. 'Brenton, I'm sorry.'

He laughed humourlessly. 'Are you? Are you really?'

'I'm sorry for *you.* I understand that feeling of helplessness.' She looked into his eyes, her words imploring. 'When there's absolutely nothing you can do to control or change a situation, oh, yes, I understand that completely.'

He raked a hand through his hair and then shoved both hands into his trouser pockets. 'So what do we do now? What have you told Lily?'

'About you?'

'Yes.'

'I've told her the truth—well, what I *believed* was the truth until today.'

'You told her I was dead.'

'Yes.'

'What about the other guy you married?'

'What about him?'

'Did she think he was her father?'

Natasha frowned. 'She was only three and a half when he died. She doesn't remember him.'

'So she's essentially reached the age of six—almost seven—years old without having a father.'

'Yes.' She smiled up into his blue eyes. 'But she has one now.'

He held her gaze before pulling out his car keys. 'I need to go, unless there are any other bombshells you'd like to drop?'

Natasha took a step back. 'No.' They both needed time to process all this new information. Oh, how she wished everything could be sorted out with a snap of the fingers. She walked him to the door. 'I guess I'll see you tomorrow.'

'I guess you will.' He waited for her to open the door before saying, 'Promise you won't say anything to Lily about me.'

'Why? She needs to find out some time. She's lived her whole life without you.'

'It's just until tomorrow. I need to think, to get my head around what's happened.'

'You don't believe me.' Natasha was surprised at how much that hurt. 'I'm not lying to you, Brenton. Lily *is* your daughter.'

He raked his hand through his hair again. 'Right now, I don't know what to believe but I do have one other question for you. Why did you call her Lily?'

'Why do you think?'

'You knew I loved that name. You knew that if we had a daughter, I wanted to call her Lily.'

'Yes, I did, which is why I called her that. It was yet another way which helped me feel closer to you.' She paused. 'We *do* have a daughter, Brenton, and she needs both her mother and her father. On the other hand, I don't want to pressure you and if you decide to have nothing to do with her, then I'll respect that decision, but either way, one day, perhaps when she's a bit older, she should be told the truth— that you're alive. She has the right to know.'

He nodded. His gaze flicked momentarily from her eyes to her lips, stopping for a brief second before returning to her eyes again. Natasha felt the tension inside begin to mount once more. The chemistry between them was as natural and as powerful as it had always been. 'Some things never change,' he murmured, before turning and walking away.

He forced himself not to look back while he climbed into his white Jaguar XJ6, started the engine and drove away. He hadn't needed to look to know she'd watched him the entire time because he'd *felt* her. He'd *felt* the way her gaze had settled over him, the way his body had instantly responded to it and how he was having a difficult time keeping himself under control.

He pulled up at a red light and hit the steering-wheel in frustration. How could what she had said tonight possibly be true? His mother would have had to go to extraordinary lengths to do what Natasha claimed she'd done. In essence, his mother had faked his death! It was absurd, ridiculous and something that only happened on television or movies.

He drove to Eastern Beach, parked the car and cut the engine. Brenton wasn't sure how long he sat there, staring out at the water in front of him. He sorted methodically through things in his mind.

'No.' He started the car and turned it in the direction of the hospital. 'Work.' He needed to be somewhere that made sense and the hospital *definitely* made sense to him. Protocols, rules and regulations. Structure and order. Why couldn't his life be the same?

Five minutes later, he was stalking through the now quiet hospital corridor towards his office when he bumped into Annie. 'What are you still doing here?' he asked.

'I've just finished catching up with my admin stuff. You?'

'I'm about to start.'

'Monty? It's a quarter to eleven!'

'So? The paperwork is still there, isn't it? I don't think it will mind that it's late.' He kept walking to his office and Annie fell into step beside him.

'Have you eaten?'

He paused momentarily and looked at her, before shrugging. 'Can't remember. Not hungry.' He unlocked his office and switched on the light. Annie came in and sat down opposite his desk. He picked up a piece of paper, made his eyes follow the words, but knew his brain wasn't capable of taking anything in right now.

'Want to talk about it?'

Brenton leaned back in his chair and rubbed his fingers across his forehead but didn't speak.

'I'll go. You probably just want to be alone in your cave. I understand.' She stood.

'Cave?'

'It's where the male species retreat to when they have problems to solve.'

'Where did you hear that?'

'Read it in a book somewhere.'

'Did the book tell you *how* they solve the problems?'

Annie sat back down, making herself comfortable. 'No, but it *did* say that a lot of men *think* they have to solve the problem, but they don't. They just have to realise that the problem is there and not ignore it.'

'Doesn't make any sense.' He shook his head.

'Didn't think you'd understand.'

'Was the book written by a man or a woman?'

'What happened with Natasha?' Annie cut straight to the chase. 'I gather you went to see her tonight?'

Brenton eyed her carefully. She had her teeth in, he realised, and he knew of old that once Annie got her teeth into something she rarely let go. He shifted in his chair and told her what Natasha had said. Annie didn't make any comments. She just nodded every so often, which reassured him he wasn't boring her.

'And then...' Brenton took a deep breath and leaned forward on his desk, his hands palms down on the blotter. 'She tells me about Lily.'

'Lily?' Annie frowned. 'Who's Lily?'

'Apparently she's my six-year-old daughter.' He watched Annie's brown eyes widen in shock and her jaw drop open, and realised he must have looked as ridiculous as this when Natasha had broken the news to him.

'You have a daughter!'

'So Natasha says.'

'Did you see her?'

'Yes, but she was sleeping.'

'What are you going to do?'

'I have no idea.' Brenton stood up and started to pace. 'OK. Let's say, for the sake of argument, that what Tash has said is the truth.'

'OK.'

'This means that I have a child—the child I so desperately wanted to have with Tash all those years ago.'

'You've already missed six years of her life.'

'What's to stop me getting involved with her?'

'Nothing, but what if Natasha *isn't* telling the truth? What if Lily *isn't* yours and what if she's just trying to get back into your life?'

'Hmm.'

'When we've talked about your ex-wife on the very few occasions you've let me into your cave, you said she'd cheated on you, packed up her things and left without a word, serving you with divorce papers—all communication being done through solicitors.'

He nodded thoughtfully. 'Now you see that's where it doesn't make sense. If she thought I was dead, why did I get divorce papers from her?'

'Good question.' Annie frowned. 'How do you know she had an affair?'

'Because my mother told me.'

'What proof did she have?'

'Circumstantial evidence. I tried to find the man my mother

said Tash had had the affair with. I couldn't. He'd just disappeared off the face of the earth—as had Tash.'

'How did you know where to look?'

'He was at med school with us. She'd even dated him for
a few months.'

'When?'

'About two years before we started going out. That was
how I got to know her. This guy was in my year, Tash was
two years behind us. After she broke up with him, Tash and
I started hanging out and studying together. Just friends.'

'Oh, sure, Monty.'

'It's true. We were friends for a long time.'

'Did she date anyone else during that time?'

'No. Not that I know of.'

'Would you have known?'

'Yes.' He nodded. 'I think so.'

'How do you know?'

'Because we spent most of our free time together.'

'But your relationship was platonic.'

'Yes. We didn't want to wreck what we had by taking it
further.'

'But you obviously did.'

Brenton looked away and smiled. 'Yes. After our first kiss,
we both knew it was the *real* thing.'

'And you got married.'

'Yes.'

'And you hadn't been dating anyone else during your platonic phase?'

'No.'

'So this guy you've mentioned is really the only person
from her past, that you know of, who dated her.'

He thought for a moment. 'Yes.'

'How long were you married?'

'Seven months, one week and three days—before I left for
South America, that is.'

He watched Annie's eyebrows raise in surprise. 'That's
very exact.'

Brenton shrugged.

'So to recap here,' Annie continued, 'your mother told you Natasha had an affair with an old boyfriend, that she'd upped and left you without another word, and you believed her?'

'What was I supposed to believe? I couldn't find her at all and, believe me, I looked. An intern friend of mine confirmed she was pregnant—'

'And that fitted in with your mother's story.'

'Yes. No one seemed to know where she'd gone.'

'And this other guy had disappeared, too.'

'At the same time. Seemed too much of a coincidence to ignore.'

'Was she interested in him?'

He raked a hand through his hair. 'I don't know. She was always nice to him.'

'She strikes me as the type of person who's nice to everyone but, then, I don't know her that well.'

'What are you getting at, Annie?'

'I just don't think you can discount anything. Keep an open mind because you never know where the future might take you.'

He thumped a hand onto the desk in frustration. 'Why did it have to turn out like this?' he growled angrily. 'Why did she have to come to *this* hospital? I mean, what were the odds, Annie? Huh? First the old director gets sick and retires early, but not before he's done all the legwork for employing the new A & E registrar.' He laughed humourlessly. 'You know, I was even glad I didn't have to bother with it, that it would be all over and done with and I could take over the position without having to worry about staffing! Hah! Half my luck.'

'You mean you would have turned her down? Have you read her résumé? She's quite an asset.'

'I know. She was brilliant in med school, too,' he grumbled, almost as though he resented it. She'd always been able to keep up with whatever he'd been studying and he'd been two years ahead of her. Her intellect was what had initially attracted him. The fact that he found her irresistibly sexy had been a bonus. No—he didn't resent her brilliance. 'I don't know what I would have done but I know I would have been better prepared for seeing her today than I was.'

'Caught you both on the hop.' Annie laughed and Brenton glared at her. 'What? There's a funny side to all of this. You just can't see it yet.'

'Get out.' He pointed to the door and Annie laughed harder. She stood and crossed to his side, giving him a hug, the smile still on her face. Brenton shook his head but once more felt the corners of his mouth tug upwards. 'Why couldn't life be simple, Annie? Why couldn't I fall in love with you? Life would have been a lot less unpredictable.'

Annie threw back her head and laughed. 'Oh, wow. What a compliment. Be still, my beating heart. Well, for starters, Monty, you're not my type and I'm not yours. Secondly, we're mates. Thirdly, on the four occasions when I met your mother, she looked at me as though I was a scummy piece of garbage and last, although by no means least, you don't love me and I don't love you. Not that way. Not the way you obviously felt for Natasha.'

The laughter had gone from her eyes and she looked at him seriously. 'Don't discount any possibility, Brenton. There could still be a happily-ever-after ending for you, but you have a few obstacles you need to jump first.'

He knew she was right and the fact that she'd called him Brenton instead of Monty was a clear indication she wasn't joking with her advice.

'What about Lily? I don't want the kid to get hurt.'

'You'll do the right thing. You always do. And right now,' she said, smothering a yawn, 'I'd better get home. I'm due on in the morning.'

'Thanks, mate.'

'Ah, you'll pay. Just you wait until I fall in love. I'll be bending your ear at every available opportunity.' She laughed as she walked out the door.

Brenton sat behind his desk and leaned back in his chair. Annie was right. He couldn't discount anything but over seven years' worth of habits were hard to break overnight. When Natasha had left him, his whole life had changed. He'd fled overseas for two years to a war zone. At that point in his life, he hadn't really cared whether he'd lived or died. Finally, when he'd returned, he'd been extremely cautious of women, less trusting, and hadn't dated at all. He'd had dinner with his mother once a week until her death but even then he'd found that a chore. True, she hadn't been the easiest woman to get along with—all right, she'd been down right controlling—but she'd been his mother.

'Work,' he told himself sternly. He wasn't here to dwell on the past—a past he couldn't change. He was here to work, where he had some control over what was happening. An hour later he put his pen down and leaned back in his chair, stretching his arms overhead. His in-tray was empty and he could already hear the groan of dismay when his secretary saw his out-tray.

At least he now felt as though he'd accomplished something today. He checked his watch—it was already Tuesday. He stood and packed his briefcase before walking to the door and switching off the light. He locked his office and strode tiredly towards the car park, yawning as he went.

It wasn't far to the two-bedroomed townhouse where he lived. In fact, it was only three blocks away from where Tash was living with her aunt—*and* their daughter.

Was it true? Was Lily really his? The questions had only been pushed aside temporarily while he'd worked but now they surfaced again, filling his mind completely. There was no denying he was still attracted to Tash. His mind knew it, his body knew it and his soul knew it. That didn't mean he loved her but as far as the physical attraction went—it was definitely still there, in both of them.

He dropped his briefcase by the door and headed straight for the bathroom, unbuttoning his shirt as he walked. It was time for sleep and as he went through his nightly routine, his thoughts kept churning.

When she'd broken down, crying, he hadn't been able to

resist pulling her into his arms, and the instant he'd done it, he'd known it had been a mistake because then he'd wanted more. He'd wanted not only to wipe her tears away but to crush his lips to hers, working through the motions which would lead them both to a very satisfactory ending. He had experienced it with her before and the memories were as vivid as though he'd made love to her yesterday.

He would start by taking her hair down, as he had on so many occasions in the past. He knew instinctively where each hairpin would be and how quickly he could dispose of them. Then he would run his fingers through her hair, revelling in the soft, silky touch. Tash would close her eyes as he lightly massaged her scalp, sometimes moaning in relaxation which only succeeded in heightening his own responses.

Brenton climbed into bed, not bothering to pull the covers up. It was still stinking hot. He laced his fingers behind his head and stared up at the ceiling. Memories from the past, one after the other, paraded through his mind and he was too exhausted to fight them.

CHAPTER FOUR

'CODE one. Code one' came a female voice over the loud-speaker.

Natasha finished writing the notes for the patient she'd just finished seeing and headed to Trauma Room 1. She washed her hands, grabbed a protective gown and slipped it over her clothes, tying the tapes at the back before walking into TR-1. She was instantly conscious of Brenton standing in the room, listening carefully to what the scribe nurse was saying about the patient as she wrote the information on a large whiteboard. She forced herself to do the same.

'Patient's name is Mr Neiman. Sixty-eight-year-old male who fell from a ladder in his back yard, impaling his left foot with the prongs on an old rusty rake.'

Natasha placed a mask over her mouth, pulled on a pair of gloves and approached the unconscious patient.

'Cross-type and match,' Brenton instructed. 'Morning, Tash. Sleep well?'

Natasha cleared her throat. 'Not particularly.' At his raised eyebrow she added, 'Too hot.' She took a look at Mr Neiman's foot. 'Three puncture wounds. Tetanus shots?' she asked.

'Still waiting on that information, Doctor,' the scribe nurse answered.

'Administer one if necessary.'

'Saline IV stat,' Brenton ordered.

'Any allergies?'

'None that we know of, but we're still getting a past medical history from his wife.'

'Pulse is rapid.'

'Oxygen, three litres.'

'What does the ambulance report say?' Natasha asked.

'He was brought in by his wife,' came the answer. 'Apparently she manoeuvred him to their car and drove him here. She didn't want to bother the ambulance people as they always have more important people to deal with.'

Natasha shook her head as she ran the end of a reflex hammer up the base of the patient's feet, being careful of the puncture wounds. Goodness knew what extra damage his wife might have done to him by moving him.

'Motor responses—medium on the left leg, weak on the right,' she called. 'Check his pulses. Full neurovascular obs,' she stated.

Brenton was by Mr Neiman's head, calling to him again but having no luck. 'Still no verbal response.' He reached for a torch and checked the man's pupils. 'What?' He checked again.

'What is it?' Natasha asked, not looking at him.

'Left pupil reacting to light.' He shone the torch in the right eye. 'Right eye fixed.'

She jerked her head up from checking Mr Neiman's legs for fractures. 'Keep checking,' she told the nurse, and moved to the man's head. 'Shine it again,' she said to Brenton. He did as she suggested. The pupil didn't dilate.

Natasha gently pressed at the base of Mr Neiman's right eyelid. The eye moved and slithered into her hand. 'Prosthesis,' she said as she turned to hand it to a nurse.

'Nice one,' Annie praised as Natasha resumed her assessment. His trousers had now been removed which made her job a lot easier.

'Patient has voided.'

'Well, at least there's nothing wrong with his bladder,' someone mumbled.

'BP's dropping,' Annie announced.

'Get that IV line in and a unit of O-negative.'

'No known allergies to medication,' the scribe nurse announced.

'Pulse in the right leg is weak, possible fracture. Requires X-ray.'

'Get ortho, general surgical and neurovascular registrars here, stat. Morphine, fifteen mg.'

'BP is still dropping.'

'Carotid pulse is thready.'

'Left pupil sluggish,' Brenton announced. 'Ready crash-cart.'

'Ready.'

The nurses finished removing Mr Neiman's upper clothing and Brenton looked closer at the side of his chest. 'What's that?' He ran his hand over a red area where a bruise would later form.

'Looks as though he fell on something.'

'Respiration is falling, Doctor.'

'Intubate. He may have punctured a 'lung.' The oxygen mask was removed from Mr Neiman's mouth and nose and soon he was intubated. 'X-ray his lungs. Tash, how's his right leg doing?' Brenton stepped away while the radiographer brought the portable X-ray machine in.

'Not good. Capillary function is poor.' She looked up at him, their gazes meeting across the crowded room. It was ridiculous. They were in the middle of a crisis but in that short glance it was as though they were back to their old selves.

'Fractured?'

'Yes.'

'Can you straighten it? We need to increase neurovascular function.' His tone was less harsh but still commanding. As soon as Brenton spoke, the orthopaedic registrar walked into the room.

'Sounds like my cue,' he muttered as he finished gowning. Natasha was glad to hand the fracture over to him.

'He's in ventricular fibrillation. Cardiac arrest is imminent,' Annie announced as all tubes and wires were quickly removed.

'Paddles charged?'

'Ready.'

'Clear!' Brenton administered the shock and a second later Mr Neiman's chest started to rise and fall of its own accord. He handed the paddles to Annie and checked the patient's left pupil. 'Reacting to light. Respiratory function?'

'BP now 100 over 60.'

'Pulse is more stable.'

'Get that IV back in and check electrolyte balance.'

'Never fear—I am here,' a tall man with blond hair announced as he walked into the room and reached for a pair of gloves as a nurse did up his gown and then his mask. 'What's the problem?' he asked Brenton.

'Possible punctured lung. X-rays are on their way.' Brenton stood back as the general surgical registrar took over. The blond giant asked a few questions before glancing down to where Natasha stood.

'Hell-o,' he said, his gaze flicking between her and the patient. 'I don't believe we've…met.' He raised his eyebrows suggestively as he said the last word.

Natasha opened her mouth to respond but Brenton beat her to it.

'How remiss of me. Paul Jamieson, meet Natasha Forest— my *wife!*'

For a split second the entire room stopped and stared at Natasha. Well, she *had* wanted to make an impression at her new hospital, she just wasn't sure this was it.

It only lasted a moment but it was enough to make Natasha's own pulse rise at Brenton's audacity. How dare he do that to her? Their marital status was of no concern to the rest of the staff and she knew the grapevine tongues would be wagging incessantly for at least the next few months.

She clenched her jaw tight and continued with her work.

'Interesting,' Paul remarked. 'Didn't know you were married, Brenton. So where have you been hiding, Natasha?' As he spoke, he continued checking Mr Neiman. Everyone around her was working, doing what they were supposed to be doing, concentrating but also listening with half an ear and waiting patiently for her answer.

'Wangaratta,' she remarked. 'The pulse in his ankle is getting stronger.'

'Here are the X-rays of the lungs,' the radiographer announced as she hurried back into the room.

'Excellent,' Paul said, waiting while they were hooked onto the X-ray viewing box.

'I need an X-ray of his right tib and fib, please,' the ortho registrar said, and Natasha breathed a sigh of relief as the rest of the staff appeared to be leaving her alone—for now.

The triage sister came into the room and spoke quietly to Brenton. He nodded. 'Tash?'

She turned to look at him and he motioned to the door. They both stripped off their protective clothing before leaving the room, secure in the knowledge that Mr Neiman was being well looked after by the different sub-specialty registrars.

'I'll catch up with you another time, Natasha,' Paul Jamieson called.

She merely nodded and followed Brenton out of the room. He was moving quite fast towards TR-2.

'Unconscious patient,' he stated, and they quickly regowned and regloved before heading to the patient's side. The paramedics had just transferred her over to the hospital bed before leaving.

'Status?' Brenton asked.

'Mariah Fairleigh. Thirty-eight-year-old female. Ambulance called for by employer. Patient was reportedly sitting and staring into space before collapsing. Regained consciousness briefly in the ambulance and was very disoriented before losing consciousness again. Previous medical history includes a car accident six months ago.'

'Notes?' Tash asked.

'They're on their way.'

'Obs.' Brenton checked Mariah's pupils. 'Pupils equal and reacting to light. ECG, EEG and IV. Complete blood work-up to start with.'

As Deb, one of the nurses, started to wind the BP cuff around the patient's arm, Mariah started to shake and twitch, the muscle contractions increasing in severity with each passing second.

'She's fitting.' Brenton stated. 'Check her airway, Tash.'

The nurses loosened her clothing and also helped protect Mariah's arms and legs so she didn't hurt herself.

'Airway is currently clear.'

'Get ready to intubate if necessary.'

'Patient's voided,' Deb announced.

'Noted.'

'Two hundred mg of phenytoin, stat,' Brenton ordered. Once the injection was drawn up and administered, Mariah began to calm down, although her body was still alternating from rigidity to relaxation.

'Tonic-clonic seizure. First muscle contractions followed by jerking,' Natasha said as she re-checked Mariah's airway and pupils. 'Airway is clear, pupils still equal and reacting to light. Mariah?' she called. 'Mariah, can you hear me?'

The patient started coughing.

'Take it easy,' Brenton soothed. 'You're in Geelong General, Mariah. You passed out at work.' Mariah opened her eyes, her gaze indicating complete confusion. 'It's all right, Mariah. I'm Dr Worthington and this is Dr Forest. You're all right now.'

Mariah tried to sit up but collapsed back.

'Dizzy?' Natasha asked.

'Yes.' It was a whisper.

'Close your eyes and relax for a moment. We're just waiting for your case notes to come up from Medical Records.'

'This is an oxygen mask, Mariah,' Natasha said as she gently placed the mask over Mariah's mouth and nose. 'Your oxygen levels are a bit low.'

Natasha put her fingers into Mariah's hands. 'Can you squeeze for me?' She did. 'Good.'

'Have you ever passed out at work before?' Brenton asked.

'No.'

'Have you ever had a seizure before?'

'No.' Mariah opened her eyes, her previously worried gaze now frantic.

'Glasgow coma scale is 15,' Natasha told Deb quietly, and the nurse noted the information. 'Mariah, is there someone we can call to let them know you're here?'

'My…my mum.'

'Your mum? Sure. Do you know her number?'

Mariah sighed, obviously exhausted from the seizure. 'My bag.'

'In your bag?' At Mariah's nod, Natasha rested her hand on the woman's shoulder. 'We'll take care of it. You rest for now.'

Natasha went in search of the co-worker who had followed the ambulance to the hospital.

'How is she?'

'She's fine now.'

'Oh, thank goodness. We were all so scared, we didn't know what to do.'

'Did you bring her bag with you?'

'Yes. One of the girls ran out with it just as I was leaving. I guess she won't be coming back to work today.'

Natasha smiled politely. 'I guess not. If I could take the bag from you, Mariah has asked for it.'

'Oh, sure.' The colleague handed the bag over. 'Uh…I guess I should get back to work, then…you know, if she's going to be OK.'

'Sure. She's in good hands.' Natasha headed back to TR-2 and as Mariah was too exhausted, Natasha managed to find the address book and, consequently, Mrs Fairleigh's phone number.

Brenton held out a report to her. EEG showed nothing out of the ordinary.

'CT scan?'

'We'll see what the blood results are.'

'Urine analysis?'

'I've ordered it. Depending on what they show, she might

need an MRI. I've paged the neurology registrar who's currently in Theatre but has asked we organise her transfer to CCU. The notes have arrived. She had a bad car accident six months ago, sustaining a head injury.'

'You think that's what caused the seizure?'

'Quite possible but we won't know until we get the results.'

'Well, if you don't need me here, I'll go see what else needs doing.'

'I'll catch up with you soon,' he said briskly.

'Why?' she asked cautiously. Did he want to have round two so soon?

He shoved one hand in his trouser pocket and straightened his back. He was annoyed, she realised. She'd seen him in this mood many times before and the intimate knowledge made her a little self-conscious. She knew his mannerisms, his likes and dislikes, who he was deep down inside, but perhaps that had all changed during the past seven years?

'I like to spend some time observing new colleagues—just to be on the safe side.' He stepped closer so their conversation wasn't overheard. The scent of his aftershave mingled with her subtle perfume and she felt her pulse rate increase. She lifted her chin in a defiant gesture, as she'd always done when she felt threatened. He could still read her body language, he realised with a start, and a pang of pain pierced through him.

'Going to fire me if you don't like my methods?'

'I just might.' He turned and stalked back over to Mariah, and Natasha quickly made her exit.

'Calm down,' she muttered to herself as she returned to the nurses' station. After taking a few deep breaths, she pushed Brenton and the emotions he evoked to the back of her mind and accepted a new patient's file.

It was almost the end of her shift when he caught up with her at the nurses' station. He took the file out of her hand and read. 'Pregnant woman in Examination Cubicle 9. Has a piece of glass in the bottom of her foot. Interesting. Let's go.'

She clenched her jaw together at his high-handedness and

realised that not everything about him had stayed the same. His arrogance had grown quite a bit. 'How's Mariah?'

'Settled in CCU and under the care of the neurology registrar.' He pulled back the curtain to EC-9 and entered. 'Hannah, I'm Brenton Worthington and this is my colleague, Natasha Forest.'

'You're thirty-four weeks,' Natasha remarked as she put the notes down. 'How are you feeling?'

'Other than quite cross at myself for being so silly, not too bad.'

'Can you tell us what happened?' Brenton asked as he washed his hands and pulled on a new set of gloves.

'I was putting away the dishes and Vince ran into me, making me drop a glass.'

'I said I was sorry, Mummy.' Vince sniffed a little indignantly as he scrambled off the bedside chair and tried to climb onto the bed. His mother winced as the bed shifted and clutched her swollen abdomen.

Natasha bent down to Vince's height and noticed that his wide eyes were red-rimmed, obviously from crying. 'My goodness, you're a big boy. How old are you, Vince?'

'Four. I can spell my name. V-I-N-C-E. Vince.'

'Well done. Do you like stickers?' He nodded earnestly. 'If you can be a good boy for me and sit nice and quiet while we fix up Mummy's foot, I'll give you some stickers as a special reward. How does that sound?'

'Great.' He let Natasha lift him back onto the chair, his little legs swing excitedly, but at least he stayed glued to the chair. The last thing they needed was a four-year-old cannoning into them just as they were about to remove a piece of glass from Hannah's foot.

Brenton was taking in everything Natasha did with the child. It was obvious she was completely at ease with him. He needed to keep busy because that way he could block out other thoughts that were starting to intrude.

'Good boy. In the meantime…' She quickly grabbed a wooden tongue depressor and drew a little picture on one end.

'You can play with this but, remember, we need you to sit nice and quietly on this chair. Can you do that?'

'Uh-huh.' He nodded again.

Natasha smiled at him before returning her attention to Hannah. Brenton had positioned a light at the end of the bed and was peering closely at the foot in question. 'I need the magnifying glasses,' he said and ripped off his gloves. 'I'll be back in a moment.'

Natasha was getting rather irritated with Brenton. He said he'd wanted to watch her work and now he was taking over completely. Typical male!

'Hey—look what I can do,' Vince said as he moved the tongue depressor in the air like an aeroplane.

Hannah shushed him but it was the look from Natasha that made the little boy stop. 'Remember you said you'd try to keep nice and quiet?'

'Oh, yeah,' he said, instantly contrite.

Hannah chuckled. 'I see you have kids. That was definitely a mother-type look you just gave him. How many do you have?'

'Just the one.' Natasha smiled but didn't go into details. Hannah was rubbing her stomach in an uncomfortable way. 'Problem?'

'No. Just a foot poking up.'

'Do you mind?' Natasha held out her hand and Hannah shrugged. She felt the baby once and then went back more thoroughly. 'When was the last time you saw your obstetrician, Hannah?'

'Oh, I haven't bothered. This is my fourth child and, you know, they get kind of run-of-the-mill.'

'So you've never had an ultrasound?'

'I had one at eighteen weeks—my GP sent me for one. I was supposed to go back and see her again, but if there'd been anything major wrong they would have told me. They didn't call...' Hannah shrugged and a moment later asked, 'Why? Do you think something's wrong?'

'Have you been having a bit of back pain recently?'

'Sure, what pregnant woman doesn't?'

'I mean within the past few hours.'

'Sure, but when Vince ran into me, he pushed me from behind into the cupboard. I was conscious of not hitting the baby and kind of bent backwards a little to compensate.'

Natasha nodded. 'Nothing abnormal before then?'

'No.'

'Found them,' Brenton said as he came back into the room holding a pair of magnifying glasses which were attached to a band that sat around the circumference of the head. He put them on before washing his hands again and pulling on some gloves.

'Would you mind if I called one of our obstetric registrars to come and have a look at you?' Natasha asked.

Hannah shook her head, a little concerned. 'No, but why? Do you think there's something wrong with the baby?'

Natasha smiled encouragingly. 'I'd just feel more comfortable if you were seen. I know this is your fourth child but each pregnancy is different and therefore each needs to be treated with the same amount of care.'

'All right, Hannah. Sit back and we'll take a look at your foot,' Brenton said as he repositioned the light.

'Hold my hand.' Hannah grabbed Natasha's hand and squeezed it. One of the nurses came in to assist Brenton for there was no way, it seemed, Hannah was going to let Natasha go.

'Hmm,' he said a moment later. 'It's gone deeper than we thought, Hannah.'

'W-what? Can you get it out? I don't need surgery or anything like that, do I?'

'I'll need to make a small incision and then suture the wound up, but I can do it right here with a local anaesthetic.'

'What does that mean?' Hannah was starting to get slightly worried and she gripped Natasha's hand tighter.

'It means we just numb the area where the glass is.'

Hannah looked up at Natasha. 'It's the best way, otherwise you'll be in a lot of pain,' Natasha advised.

'All right.' Hannah bit her lip and nodded.

Brenton took off his gloves and then the glasses, a smile fixed in place. 'Let me get things organised.' He disappeared again and Hannah turned wild eyes to Natasha.

'Am I going to be OK?'

'Sure you are.'

'Can I move now?' Vince wanted to know.

'In a moment, sweetheart,' Natasha said as she turned and ruffled his hair. 'You've been very good so far so I'll see if I can find those stickers I promised you.' She turned back to Hannah. 'You may want to call someone to come and help with Vince as we'll need you to stay here for at least four hours' observation after the procedure.'

'Four hours? But the kids will be finishing school and I have to get dinner ready and—'

'I understand,' Natasha interrupted. 'Believe me, I do, but it will just have to wait. Now, who would you like me to call?'

'Uh…call my husband…' Hannah let go of Natasha's hand so she could write down the number '…and one of my friends. She'll be able to get the kids from school.' She gave Natasha the details.

'There you go, just a little bit of restructuring and it's all done. I'm sure your husband can take care of dinner.'

'Yeah, a pizza or something.'

Natasha smiled. 'I'll go give him a call. Vince…' She held out her hand to him. 'Would you like to come for a walk with me and we'll see if we can find you those stickers?'

'Cool!' He bounded off the chair and immediately took her hand.

'We won't be long,' Natasha said, leaving Hannah with the nurse. 'Let's go to the nurses' station and ask about those stickers. I know they have them around here somewhere. All hospitals have stickers for good children.' She asked one of the nurses about the stickers and, sure enough, stickers were produced. Once Vince had three of them in his hot little hands, Natasha called Hannah's husband. With that job done, she called the hospital switchboard and asked that they page the obstetric registrar. She informed the nurses about Hannah's condition so they knew what was going on.

Annie walked back in and was more than willing to entertain Vince for ten minutes to keep him out of the examination cubicle while the glass was removed from Hannah's foot.

When Natasha returned to EC-9, Brenton was just finishing injecting the local anaesthetic. The nurse's hand was being turned purple by Hannah, and the instant it was over Natasha said, 'BP, resp, pulse.' The nurse nodded, obviously glad to get her hand back. 'How's the back pain, Hannah?'

'Getting worse. Did you get through to my husband?'

'Yes. He'll contact your friend and organise the other children. Vince is showing the nurses his new stickers.'

Hannah smiled but it ended up being more of a grimace. Natasha crossed to Brenton's side. 'Hannah's been experiencing a bit of discomfort,' she murmured quietly. 'I've put in a page for the obstetrics registrar to come and check her out.'

'Your hunch?'

'Breech.'

He nodded. 'Your hunches used to be spot on. Hannah, would you mind if I feel your abdomen?'

'No. Why?'

'I'd just like to have a feel.'

'It's all right, Hannah,' Natasha soothed. 'Your baby is fine, it just feels as though he hasn't turned yet.'

'Oh.' Hannah relaxed. 'Is that all? All of my others were late turners but they all got there in the end.'

'How many children do you have?' Brenton asked.

'This is my fourth.'

Brenton felt Hannah's abdomen and nodded to Natasha. 'You were right.'

The nurse reported the observation results and jotted them down in the notes. Hannah's BP was on a slight incline but nothing too bad at the moment.

'Where you thought you felt the baby's foot before, it was really the shoulder,' Natasha explained as she checked for swelling in Hannah's ankles and then her hands. 'No swelling, that's good.'

'How's the foot feeling? Tingly? Numb?' Brenton asked.

'I can't feel it. Am I wiggling my toes? I can't see them any more,' she added wryly.

'Let's see what's happening.' Brenton felt the area but received no response. He did a quick test but again there was no response. 'Good. Looks as though we're ready to start.'

They pulled on gowns, masks and gloves before starting the procedure. Brenton concentrated on the task at hand and not too long after managed to remove the offending sliver of glass.

'Looks as though you're having a lot of fun in here,' a female voice said from behind them. Brenton glanced over his shoulder.

'Hi, Carol. We're almost done here.'

Natasha washed out the area to make sure there weren't any other bits of glass embedded in Hannah's foot as Carol introduced herself to Hannah as the obstetrics registrar. When both Brenton and Natasha were satisfied with the wound site, Brenton put in a couple of neat stitches.

'Good as new,' he said, and glanced at his patient.

'Thanks, both of you…and for looking after Vince.'

'I'll ask the nurse to bring him back if you like,' Natasha offered.

'Thanks.'

'We'll leave you in Carol's capable hands,' Brenton said, and together he and Natasha walked out.

'Arrange for Vince to be returned to his mother and meet me in my office. Five minutes, Tash.' With that he stalked off.

A bit perplexed, Natasha did as he asked and was knocking on his office door in under the five minutes.

'Come in,' he called briskly. When she poked her head around he said, 'Close the door.'

She did as he asked and crossed towards him. 'Something wrong?'

'Yes.' He stood and came around his desk. 'You should leave the care of any of the patients' children to the nursing staff.'

'Excuse me?'

'You heard.'

'I did what I needed to do to defuse the situation. I could tell Hannah was getting agitated with Vince which wasn't helping, either herself or the baby.'

'And I suppose you know this because you're a mother?'

'That's right.' She watched him closely as he crossed his arms over his chest. 'Look, I can't help it that I've had a child for almost seven years, Brenton, so stop punishing me for it.'

'I was talking about the level of your patient care.'

'Really? Didn't sound that way to me.'

'*I* was supposed to be watching *you* work and instead *I* ended up doing everything.'

'What? You muscled your way in is more like it. I just got to stand there and pass you instruments.'

'That's absurd.'

'What's absurd, B.J., is your behaviour.'

Before she could say another word, he'd closed the gap between them and hauled her into his arms. She was positive her heart rate had skipped several beats and as he stared down at her, his breath coming out hard and fast, excitement zinged through her veins.

'How do you expect me to react? Hmm?' His words were fierce yet hungry. 'All day long I've struggled to keep you tucked into the far recesses of my mind, but it isn't working. Your perfume drives me insane, the sway of your hips mesmerises me when you walk, and if you look at me with those wide and luscious green eyes—just as you're doing now—I won't be held responsible for my actions.'

His words only increased the tension flooding through her and as she parted her lips, wetting them with her tongue, she was also conscious of the knock at his door.

He dropped her like a hot potato and strode away, raking

his hand through his hair. 'Stay,' he commanded her, before calling, 'Come in.'

Natasha glanced away as his secretary came in with a pile of files. 'I'm leaving for the day, Brenton,' she said as she dumped the files into his in-tray. 'Try not to stay too late. Goodnight.'

Natasha looked up briefly but didn't meet the other woman's eyes. She couldn't. Had his secretary any idea of what had just transpired in this office? When the door closed behind them, she sank down into a chair.

'We've got to sort this out,' she muttered. 'The past, the attraction we both feel... We can't go on like this, Brenton! It will tear us both apart.'

CHAPTER FIVE

'YOU'RE right, and it's got to be soon because you're filling my thoughts way too much and...' He trailed off. 'You know, let's not go there just now. I wanted to talk to you about Lily. I've thought about things.' He rubbed his fingers across his forehead. 'You. Her. This entire situation seems to be all I can think about and, anyway, I've come to the decision that I'd like to meet her.'

'Are you sure? Do you still have doubts that you're her father?'

'I won't lie to you, Tash, but, yes, I do.'

'She's your daughter, Brenton. You'll realise that the instant you see her.'

'Do you have a picture?'

She smiled. 'Only her baby picture. It's in my wallet. I can get it if you like.'

He shook his head. 'It's all right.'

'I know you don't trust me, Brenton, and I know it's probably due to things your mother has obviously said about me, but why would I lie to you in this instance? Why would I pretend Lily is your child? Just so I can get her a father?' Natasha shook her head before answering her own question. 'She's basically been without a father all her life and, quite frankly, she's doing just fine. The reason I've told you is because you are her father, Brenton. *You* have a right to know of her existence, just as she has a right to know of yours.'

He nodded slowly, his gaze determined. 'You're right. I do want to meet her and I guess I'm going to have to trust you in this instance and believe you. But if you've lied...'

'I haven't.' Her words were firm and true.

'OK. So, as I'm completely out of my depth here, how do you suggest we tell her?'

'Well, for a start, I suggest that *I* tell her and for you to see her once she's had time to get used to the idea.' He was about to open his mouth to protest but Natasha rushed on. 'I don't want her to go through the shock I'm still coming to terms with. She's only six and if I can protect her, I will.'

He frowned and thought for a moment before saying, 'All right. Let me know when it's done.'

'I will.'

Brenton crossed his arms over his chest and Natasha tried not to be distracted by the muscles flexing beneath his white cotton shirt. 'I'm happy to become involved in Lily's life. I'd like to see her as much as possible so we'll need to figure out the best way to do that.'

'Agreed.' Natasha stood. 'I'll tell Lily tonight.'

He face was grim. 'Thank you.'

Once Natasha was finished at the hospital she drove home on autopilot, parking the car before heading inside, her mind still whirling with everything that had happened during the past twenty-four hours. If Mrs Worthington had gone to such extraordinary lengths to convince her that Brenton had died in South America, heaven only knew what she'd done to convince him that she had no longer wanted to spend her life with him.

Lily and Aunt Jude had already eaten and Natasha quickly changed out of her work clothes so she could supervise Lily's homework.

'Read the words that are there, Lil,' she said with an exasperated sigh when Lily kept looking at the picture and guessing rather than sounding out the word.

'She's doing a good job,' Aunt Jude butted in.

'Have you had a bad day, Mum?' Lily put her arms around her mother's neck and planted a kiss on her cheek.

'Sort of. Why? Am I being grumpy?'

'Sort of,' Lily replied with a smile.

Natasha hugged Lily close, relaxing a little. 'Lil,' she said softly, 'does it bother you that you don't have a daddy?' The steady click-clack of Aunt Jude's knitting needles punctured the stillness.

'Sometimes.' Lily snuggled in to her and she kissed her head. 'I think it might be nice to go to a park and play or have him carry me on his shoulders.' She was quiet for a moment. 'Why did my real daddy die?'

Pain shot through Natasha at the question. It wasn't the first time she'd had to answer it and even though Lily's memory was getting longer so she now remembered the answers, the actual processing of information was still rather slow.

Now, though, there was a different answer to that question. It would be a complete contradiction for Lily and Natasha prayed her daughter was strong enough to comprehend it. 'Well...remember I told you that daddy had to go and work in another country and that there was a lot of people fighting in that country?'

'Yes, and he got hurt and died.'

'Well, that's what Mummy was told.'

'Who told you?'

'Your dad's mother.'

'Hey, we learnt about this in school today. If she is my dad's mother then she's my grandmother.' Lily's eyes were alive with knowledge.

'That's right. Good girl.'

'Where is she now?'

'She died, honey.'

'Oh. Just like my dad.'

'Well actually...' Natasha glanced across at Aunt Jude who nodded encouragingly. 'Mummy had a bit of a...surprise yesterday.'

'Why? What happened, Mum?' Lily was a bit concerned. Aunt Jude's needles stopped. Silence filled the room.

'Uh...I found out that your daddy didn't really die.' Tears welled in Natasha's eyes.

'He didn't?' Lily's eyes were as wide as saucers. 'Why not?'

'His mum—your grandma—made a...a mistake.'

'So I've got a dad?'

'Yes.'

'And he's really alive and not dead?'

'That's right.' Natasha's eyes shimmered with tears, her chin wobbling a bit as she smiled at her daughter.

'Cool.' The knitting needles started again. 'Do you know where he is?'

'Uh…yes.' Natasha wiped the tears from her eyes. 'He works at the hospital with me.'

'He's a doctor, too? Oh, yeah, I remember now. You've told me before he was a doctor just like you.'

'That's right. Well, he would…um…like to come over and play with you…some time.'

'Really?' Lily's blue eyes were wide with surprise and happiness. 'This is so cool. When?'

'Um…he didn't say but I can ask him tomorrow.'

'Can we call him? Why can't we call him now?'

Natasha stared at Aunt Jude who merely shrugged. She didn't want to squash Lily's enthusiasm but wasn't sure whether this was a good idea.

'He could come over tomorrow after school and play—well, if he's not working,' Lily said, obviously remembering he was a doctor. 'Come on, Mum.' Lily squirmed out of the embrace and tugged at Natasha's hand. 'Let's call him, *now*.'

'I don't have his home number, Lil.'

'Maybe he's still at the hospital?' Aunt Jude offered.

'Ring the hospital, Mummy. That's where he is, I just know it.'

'All right. We'll try the hospital but if we can't talk to him tonight, I'll ask him to come over for dinner tomorrow.' There was no way Lily was going to get to sleep tonight until it was all arranged.

'OK.'

Natasha carried the portable handset into the room and sat back down. She'd preprogrammed the hospital's number into the phone the previous week and as she pressed the preset button, she realised she was shaking. 'Er…hi,' she said to the switchboard operator. 'This is Dr Forest, Natasha Forest. I started as an A & E registrar yesterday and I was wondering if you could try Dr Worthington's extension to see if he's still in his office.' There was a click and then a ringing sound.

'Hey, his name is Worthington and so is mine,' Lily squealed delightedly as she bounded around beside her mother.

'Dr Worthington.' Brenton's deep voice startled her and momentarily she couldn't speak. 'Hello?'

'Uh…Brenton.'

'Tash.' She could hear the impatience in his tone.

'Let me talk, Mum. Let me talk.' Lily was almost ripping the receiver out of her hand and Natasha just let it go.

'Hello?' Lily said excitedly into the receiver. 'Is this my dad?'

Natasha held her breath, watching her daughter's face expectantly, praying that everything would be all right and that she hadn't just exposed Lily to the biggest hurt of her life. The huge smile on Lily's face grew even more and Natasha could hear Brenton's deep tone but couldn't make out what he was saying.

'It's so cool,' Lily remarked. 'Do you know that your name is Worthington and so is mine? We're learning all about families at my new school and now I can tell my teacher that I have a dad. Hey, guess what? Well, Josephine who sits next to Timmy, who smells really yucky so I'm glad I'm not sitting next to him, well, Josephine told me that she didn't have a dad either and now I've got one, maybe I can share you with her and then she can have one too because it's really good to share. Hey, guess what? I'm learning to read and today we played a running game at lunchtime and I could run faster than Josephine but Timmy runs faster than both of us but that's OK because he's a boy and anyway I almost catched him.'

'Caught,' Natasha automatically corrected.

'Caught him,' Lily repeated, and continued. 'You can come over tomorrow, you know. Mum said you could come for dinner and play after school if you're not working, but if you are, you could come another day. I know what you look like because Mummy has a picture of you in a silver frame in her underwear drawer—'

'Lily!' Natasha snatched the phone back off her daughter, her face blushing bright red. Thank goodness Brenton couldn't see her, especially as she could hear his deep chuckles coming from the receiver.

'What, Mum?'

'Come on, Miss Muffet,' Aunt Jude said, putting down her knitting. 'Time for you to get ready for bed.'

'I want to say goodbye to him.' She held out her hand for the phone. 'Bye, Daddy. I'll see you tomorrow.' And she blew a kiss down the phone before handing it back to Natasha and bouncing off with her aunt, chanting, 'I've got a daddy. I've got a daddy.'

'I'll come and tuck you in,' Natasha called. She took two deep breaths and cleared her throat before putting the phone to her ear. 'Hi.'

'That obviously went well.' Laughter now replaced his earlier impatience.

'Yes.' Natasha shook her head, still bemused by Lily's reaction.

'Kids just accept, Tash,' he said, as though he could read her mind.

'Why can't we?' she whispered.

'Too much history,' he said after a while. 'I didn't realise her surname was Worthington.'

'Why wouldn't it be? She *is* your daughter, Brenton. I know you think I've done all sorts of horrible things—I have no idea what they are but I can just imagine what your mother made up about me and it's *those* things, Brenton, that broke your heart. You think I deserted you but I didn't. You think I divorced you but I don't remember signing any divorce papers. Lily *is* a Worthington and I know you'll realise that when you see her. She's so much like you. You have the exact same shaped eyes as well as colour.'

'Was that hard for you? I mean if she really looks like me, didn't that bring back bad memories?'

'On the contrary. I'd look at Lily and be glad I still had something from our life together other than *wonderful* memories.'

He was silent again and she started to feel uncomfortable. 'So I've been invited around for dinner tomorrow night?'

'That's right. She insisted we ring you and now she's desperate to meet you. Can you make it?'

'Of course.' Silence again. 'Tash?'

'Yes?'

'What are you wearing?'

Warmth spread over her at his words and she closed her eyes, leaning back against the lounge cushions for support. 'B.J.,' she warned, and was surprised to find her tone breathless. It was a silly game they'd played when they'd first got married. Brenton had been working as an intern and Natasha had been furiously studying to pass her final year of medicine. Some nights apart were longer than others and he would call her during one of his breaks and ask her what she was wearing.

'Sorry, I couldn't help it. Sitting here at work, talking to you on the phone. Old habits die hard, especially when you call me B.J. I like the way you say it.' He paused. 'So, are you going to answer the question?'

She could hear the desire in his voice and realised her heart was pounding furiously against her ribs. Her lips were suddenly dry and it had nothing to do with the air-conditioner. How did he still have the ability to get her completely aroused with just one little question?

She cleared her throat and licked her lips. 'My feet are…bare. My knees are…bare.' She couldn't help the huskiness of her voice. 'My thighs àre…bare. My hands are…bare. My elbows are…bare. My shoulders are…almost bare. They have shoestring straps which are attached to my white satin camisole. Below that is a pair of white satin boxer shorts.'

'And your hair?' His tone was raspy and filled with desire.

She fluffed her fingers through it. 'Loose and curling slightly in the humidity.' He moaned in frustration and she laughed, amazed she still had the power to affect him. It was heady stuff.

'Do you really have a photograph of me in your underwear drawer?'

'Yes. One of you on our wedding day.'

He exhaled harshly. 'I've got to go. See you tomorrow.' He slammed the receiver down without another word and rested his head back against his chair, his eyes closed tightly. Why had he even started? What had possessed him to ask the opening question in the first place? She still knew how to play the game and he remembered when she'd been studying, he'd made her answer the question using the correct bone names as well as naming the muscles that surrounded each bone. Concentrating on the medical aspect rather than the physical aspect had been the only way he had been able to get through his shifts!

He sat forward in his chair, placing his elbows on the desk and burying his face in his hands before sliding his fingers into his hair. She still had a photograph of him. She still kept a photograph of him! Wasn't that a good sign?

He shifted in his chair again and pulled his wallet from his back trouser pocket. He opened it and dug down into a secret back compartment, pulling out a photograph of a woman dressed in white. Brenton gazed down into Natasha's laughing eyes. *His* Tash. *His* wife. 'Snap!'

Natasha furiously brushed her hair, secured it in a band and wound it into a bun at the nape of her neck, holding the pins between her lips as the light turned green. She put the car in motion and prayed for another set of red lights. Although they were making her later than she already was, it would allow her to finish doing her hair and make-up.

She couldn't believe she'd slept in. Aunt Jude had organised Lily with breakfast and getting ready for school. Natasha hadn't found sleep until the early hours of the morning which was why she'd overslept.

The light turned to orange and she slowed down, winding her hair back into the bun and securing it with the pins. Next she pulled out her mascara and managed to get that on before the light turned to green.

The rest of the lights were green but as there was only her lipstick to do, she didn't mind doing that after she'd parked her car. Thank goodness it wasn't too far from her aunt's house to the hospital and at least she now looked more presentable than half an hour ago when she'd woken up.

After slapping on some lipstick, she hurried through the corridors towards A & E, ten minutes late for her shift. She quickly put her things in her locker and grabbed her stethoscope. Brenton was just coming out of a treatment room with Paul Jamieson when he caught sight of Natasha.

He made a point of looking at his watch, the scowl on his face a clear indication that her absence had been noticed.

'Well, don't you look gorgeous?' Paul drawled. His gaze flickered over Natasha's knee-length brown skirt and russet top. Brenton's scowl deepened.

'Finally decided to show up,' he growled.

'Sorry,' she apologised, telling herself he had a right to be annoyed, especially as it looked as though they were busy.

'That's an interesting way to talk to your *wife*,' Paul commented. 'Are you sure you two are really married?'

'Any particular reason why you were late?' Brenton ignored Paul's comment and picked up another set of case notes, glancing at her expectantly. She could tell by his tone that he was trying to be obtuse, to rile her and make her cross. She refused to rise to the bait and shrugged nonchalantly.

'The usual cry of a mother.' Natasha noticed Paul's look turn from interested to disinterested in a split second. Good. 'Some mornings run more smoothly than others and at the moment Lily is making quite a lot of…adjustments to her life. Things are bound to be a bit difficult.' She tried not to smile smugly at Brenton's contrite expression. 'Are those case notes for me?' she asked, and accepted them with thanks before walking off, her chin held high.

She saw a steady stream of patients, her path rarely crossing Brenton's, for the rest of the morning. Heat exhaustion, sunburn, one elderly woman who was severely dehydrated. Just before lunch, she dropped by his office, hoping to talk to him about Lily, but his secretary told her he was in a meeting. She just wanted to check that everything was still all right for their dinner that evening.

'Natasha.' She turned to see Annie walking towards her. 'Patient in TR-2 just brought in via ambulance.' She handed Natasha the notes.

'Thanks. Are you coming, too?'

'Sure, why not?'

'Laceration to right arm,' Natasha murmured as she read the notes. 'She was up a ladder, cleaning a window, and lost her balance, fell through a set of glass doors and ended up with a piece of glass sticking out of her right forearm.' She walked into TR-2 and put the case notes down before washing her hands, pulling on a pair of gloves and crossing to the patient's side. 'Hi, there, Felicity. I'm Dr Natasha Forest and I'll be helping you out here. Who called the ambulance for you?'

'My neighbour. He heard the loud crash and came over to investigate.'

'Just as well he did. Did you take anything for the pain? Paracetamol?'

'No. He helped me up and gave me a drink while we waited for the ambulance.'

'What did you drink?'

'Just water. Is that all right?'

'Sure. That's great. Now, you say your right arm is where the worst cut is, so let's have a look.' Natasha crossed around to Felicity's right side as Annie and an intern finished helping Felicity remove her top. 'We'll get you into a trendy hospital gown in a minute,' Natasha said with a smile. 'All right, now.' She took off the bandage the paramedics had put on. 'That's not too bad,' she said. 'It's just over one centimetre long and doesn't look to be too deep, so that's good.' Natasha touched the region gently and Felicity almost went through the roof. 'Was there an actual piece of glass stuck into your arm or did it come out immediately?'

'My neighbour pulled it out.'

'OK. We need to make sure there aren't any tiny bits of glass in your arm so we'll get that organised. Anywhere else that really hurts?'

'Besides all over?' Felicity replied on a half-laugh.

Natasha smiled. 'I can well believe it. You'll feel the bruises over the next few days and will be a bit stiff and sore, but for the most part I think you'll do fine.'

'BP and temperature are normal,' Annie reported.

'Thanks. Felicity, are your immunisations up to date?'

'I had a tetanus injection when I was ten. That's about the last one I remember having,' Felicity said after a few moment's thought.

'And how old are you now?'

'Twenty-three.'

'All right. We'll add a tetanus shot to the list, then.' Natasha nodded at Annie who acknowledged the comment. 'First of all, I'll give you a local anaesthetic in your arm to numb the area where I'll be working.'

'I don't have to have an operation or anything like that?'

'No.' Natasha shook her head. 'We should be able to sort you out right here so let's get started.' She administered the local, and while they were waiting for it to take effect she cleaned the external area. Once the anaesthetic had done its job, Natasha debrided the wound, irrigating it to ensure there were no glass particles left. When she was satisfied, she packed the wound and bandaged it.

'Don't I need to have stitches?' Felicity asked.

'No. We need the wound to heal from the inside out so you'll need to have it cleansed and bandaged regularly at least for the next seven to ten days. The district or home nurses will do that for you,' Natasha explained as she wound a bandage around the arm. 'I'm going to give you an injection of antibiotic to start you off, but I'll write you out a prescription for tablets which you must take, otherwise you'll be risking infection.'

Natasha wrote up the treatment notes and the requests for the antibiotics and tetanus medication.

'Thanks, Dr Forest,' Felicity said.

'My pleasure.' As Natasha left TR-2, she glanced at the clock on the wall. Lunchtime—she was starving.

'Hey—free for lunch?' Annie asked as she caught up with Natasha on the way to the cafeteria.

'Sure.' Natasha was interested to find out just how good a friend Annie was with Brenton. Were they dating? Annie hadn't mentioned anything and seemed to know about *their* past connection.

Once they were seated, their food in front of them, Natasha decided to come right to the point. 'Annie, you said you and Brenton were friends.'

'That's right. We've known each other since high school but then we lost touch for about ten years.'

'Did you ever date?'

'Monty and me? No way.' She shuddered. 'No. We're not romantically suited at all.' Annie gave a theatrical sigh. 'I don't seem to be compatible with love.' She turned her gaze to Natasha, her tone soft. 'You, however, seem to have been given another chance.'

'I'm not so sure about that. So you are just *friends* with Brenton,' she stated, wanting to make sure she had it right.

'There's nothing romantic between us, Natasha.' Annie hesitated for a second. 'But he does confide in me. I know about your marriage and he told me about your daughter.'

'When?'

'Monday night.'

Natasha nodded. 'He came back to the hospital to work. To lose himself. Typical males. Back in their caves.'

'Yep. That's what I said.' The two women laughed. Natasha's pager beeped and she read the extension number.

'A & E?'

'Yes,' she mumbled as she took another bite of her sandwich and stood. 'I'll see you later.'

When she arrived back in A & E, chewing the last bite of her sandwich, the triage nurse handed her a file. 'Mrs Berry in TR-2. Seventy-four-year-old woman, brought in via ambulance due to pain when breathing.'

'Thanks.' Natasha washed her hands, pulled on a protective gown and headed into TR-2.

'Good afternoon, Mrs Berry. I'm Dr Forest.' Natasha scanned the ambulance report quickly, noting the patient had received oxygen which had eased her pain slightly. 'We're going to get you sorted out right now.' She manoeuvred her stethoscope into her ears as the nurse lifted Mrs Berry's stylish silk shirt up. She listened closely to the heart and chest before removing her stethoscope from her ears. 'Have you been sick in the past few months? Lung infection? Coughing? Wheezing?' When the woman didn't respond, Natasha said, 'It's all right. You can talk while the oxygen mask is on.'

'Not really.' The answer was clipped and to the point.

'Nothing at all? It says in your notes that you've been taking cough medicine recently.'

'Yes. I'd like to see Dr Worthington, please. I understand *he's* the one in charge around here.'

Natasha's eyebrows shot up momentarily at the request before she smiled politely. 'I'm afraid Dr Worthington is in a meeting.'

'I'll wait.'

Natasha kept the smile in place. 'It may be at least another hour.'

'I'll wait,' she said more forcefully.

Not wanting to distress the patient, Natasha continued. 'I'll have him paged for you immediately.' She nodded to the nurse who picked up a hospital phone and carried out her request. 'In the meantime, we can at least get you a little more comfortable and perhaps find out what seems to be the trouble.'

'I don't want *you* treating me.' Mrs Berry was getting quite upset now.

'I'm sorry?' Natasha was surprised. 'Is there a problem?'

'You're a home-wrecker. Did you think I wouldn't recognise you?'

'I think you have me confused with someone else.'

'Natasha Gilford or whatever your name was back then. Oh, I remember you very well.'

Natasha felt the colour drain from her face. Who *was* this woman?

'You destroyed young Brenton's life. Running off with that other man. No. I *won't* let you treat me.' Mrs Berry was becoming even more agitated.

Natasha glanced uncomfortably across at the nurse, who was trying to appear disinterested. The phone in the room rang and Natasha was relieved when the nurse said it was Brenton. 'Thanks.' Natasha took the receiver. 'Continue with neurological obs,' she instructed the nurse before turning her attention to the phone. 'Sorry to disturb you, Brenton, but there's a Mrs Berry here who says she'd like to see you. She's been brought in via ambulance with a respiratory problem.'

'Has she been giving you a hard time?' His tone was impatient and annoyed.

'That's correct.'

'She was a good friend of my mother's.'

'Ah.' The fog was clearing.

'I'll be right there. Continue with initial treatment.'

Natasha replaced the receiver and returned to Mrs Berry's side. 'Dr Worthington is on his way but has asked that I continue with initial treatment until he arrives. Obs?' she asked the nurse.

'Pulse is normal. Temperature is slightly increased. BP is 110 over 80.'

Natasha washed her hands again and pulled on a pair of gloves before picking up a tongue depressor and medical torch. 'If I could just check inside your mouth, Mrs Berry, it would help Dr Worthington's assessment.' The patient rolled her eyes heavenward but didn't protest when Natasha removed the oxygen mask to check inside Mrs Berry's mouth. She asked her to say 'ah' before replacing the mask.

'ECG to check her heart rate,' she requested as she took off her gloves. 'Well, the good news, Mrs Berry, is there's no problem with your throat. When I listened to your chest, I heard a rubbing sort of sound whenever you breathed in. This is usually an indication of an inflammation in the lungs, which was why I asked you if you'd been wheezing or coughing.' She reached for the notes and started to write down her findings. 'I'd like you to have a chest X-ray to confirm this diagnosis and to make sure the inflammation hasn't spread. I'd also like you to have a blood test so we can check your oxygen and carbon dioxide levels as well as your haemoglobin count.'

'I would prefer Dr Worthington to make those assessments. I don't trust you and, quite frankly, I don't know how *he* could stand to see you again. You should be fired. My husband is on the board of directors so we'll just see how long you last here.'

Natasha steeled herself against the attack, forcing the wall that had slowly broken down over the years back in place to protect herself. She also reminded herself that the patient needed to remain calm, but in between difficult breaths it appeared Mrs Berry was determined to have her say.

'You broke his heart, you know, you worthless hussy. Angelica had been right about you all along. If only he'd listened to his mother, he would never have married the likes of you.'

'That's quite enough,' Brenton said firmly yet quietly as he walked into the room. 'My relationship with Natasha is none of your business or anyone else's for that matter. You look terrible, Aunty Beryl.' He gave her cheek a polite peck before accepting the notes from Natasha. He read them quickly. 'That's fine.' He nodded. 'Write up the requests.' Natasha carried out his orders while he listened to Mrs Berry's chest and checked her throat.

She was about to leave him to it when he said conversationally, 'Dr Forest is an excellent registrar with good credentials. Geelong General is very lucky to have her, so if you're thinking of getting Uncle John to throw some weight around with the hospital board, think again. I stand behind her one hundred per cent and will gladly say as much to any board of enquiry, not that Natasha would require one.' He glanced across and smiled at her. It was the first real smile she'd received from him since her sudden re-emergence into his life. Her knees started to buckle and she quickly reached a hand out to the wall for support. The smile was powerful and her increased heart rate was testimony to it.

Without having a clue how he affected her, Brenton ripped off the ECG reading and nodded approvingly before handing it to Natasha, his fingers lightly brushing her own. It was enough to send a wave of tingles spreading throughout her entire body.

'The ECG is fine but I'd like to leave it on for a bit longer so we can monitor for heart arrhythmias. Set up an IV to keep fluids under control.' He reached for the notes and scribbled something down in his usual illegible scrawl before nodding. 'I'll see you when you're finished in X-Ray,' he said, and gave Beryl another token peck on the cheek. 'Tash.' He nodded as he walked out. She looked over at Beryl, who was lying back with her eyes closed while the nurse set up the IV.

'Page me if there's anything else,' Natasha said, before heading back to the nurses' station, ready for her next patient. It was nice that Brenton had supported her professionally and it made her immensely happy to know he was proud of her accomplishments.

He'd looked calm and relaxed when he'd walked into the treatment room yet all day long she'd been wondering if things would be even more awkward between them after their phone conversation last night. She hadn't slept well, although it had been marginally better than the night before.

One more hour and the day would be done. Well, her working day at any rate. With Brenton coming over for dinner, who knew *what* would unfold?

CHAPTER SIX

JUST outside the hospital, Natasha switched on her mobile phone and found she had a message. It was from Aunt Jude, asking her to pick up a few extra supplies on the way home, so she headed towards the shopping centre. When she arrived home she dumped the shopping bags in the kitchen and rushed to her bedroom to change. They were having an early dinner because both Aunt Jude and Natasha wanted to keep Lily's routine as much on track as possible. Then again, it wasn't every day a six-year-old girl found out her father wasn't dead, so they had to give her some leeway.

'How do I look?' Natasha asked as Lily wandered into her bedroom.

'All dressed up. Where are you going?' she asked indignantly. 'I thought we were having dinner *here!*'

Natasha surveyed the little black dress in the mirror. 'You're right. Definitely too dressy.' She slipped out of it and rummaged in her wardrobe for something else. 'Too dressy. Too sloppy.'

'It's just my *dad,* Mum.'

'She's right,' Aunt Jude said from the doorway. 'Just put on a pair of shorts and a top and come and give me a hand in the kitchen. Lily, you can set the table.'

'OK. What time did he say he'd be here?' she asked her mother anxiously as she bounced off the bed.

'Six o'clock on the dot.'

'Did he promise?'

Natasha thought for a moment, knowing how important this was to six-year-olds. 'I don't think he said the actual words but I do know he was very excited. Off you go and do your job.' It was true. She'd bumped into him before leaving the

76

hospital. He'd apologised again for Beryl Berry, informing Natasha that the diagnosis had been pleurisy and that she had been admitted before being transfered to a private hospital.

He'd taken a step closer and in a more intimate tone, which had caused goose-bumps to ripple out over her entire body, had said he was looking forward to tonight. Surely that translated into 'excited' in six-year-old language.

Soon everything was done and the butterflies in Natasha's stomach were now so out of control she doubted she'd be able to eat anything. When the doorbell rang, Lily squealed with delight and bounded down the hallway calling loudly, 'I'll get it. I'll get it.' She stopped and paused at the front door, her hands on the locks as she looked over her shoulder at Natasha. Completely excited she might be, but at least she'd remembered the rule about not opening the door without her mother's or aunt's permission.

'OK.' Natasha nodded as she continued down the hallway and Lily quickly opened the wooden door. She bounced around as she unlocked the screen door as well, pushing it open.

Brenton took a few steps back so he didn't get hit in the face by a swinging door before slowly crouching down to Lily's height.

The little girl needed no more of an invitation and threw her arms around his neck, burying her face there. 'It's you. It's you,' she said over and over. 'It's really you. I just can't believe it.'

Brenton put one hand around the small body which was pressed firmly against his own. He felt the warmth of her back beneath her pink cotton T-shirt. He breathed in deeply as though wanting to savour every moment.

He closed his eyes briefly as pure love swelled in his heart. When he opened his eyes again, he looked up at Natasha. She'd been right. If he'd had any doubt before about Lily's parentage, he didn't now. She had her mother's auburn hair but he could tell it would grow darker with age. Her mouth, the brief glimpse he'd caught of it before she'd hurled herself into his arms, had been curved into a smile that matched his own but her eyes…they were identical in shape and colour to his own. They were a Worthington genetic trait.

He felt a lump rise in his throat and tears blurred his vision temporarily as the truth hit home with force.

He had a child!

Lily was *his* daughter!

He tried to stand but found Lily's arms were glued to him. His only option was either to put her from him, which he wasn't at all sure he wanted to do, or pick her up. Rising to his feet, he hoisted her into his arms and held her securely, the crinkling of Cellophane making Lily's eyes widen in pleasure.

'What's that?'

'Flowers,' he replied as he settled the bouquet in her arms.

'For *me?*'

He laughed. 'Who else would I give lilies to?'

'Check this out, Mum.' Lily held her flowers proudly and possessively as she beamed from ear to ear. 'Daddy gave me *flowers*. They're lilies, just like my name.'

Natasha smiled, wiping the tears from her eyes and sniffing a little. 'They're beautiful, darling. Why don't we put them in a vase?'

'Yes.' Lily squirmed in Brenton's arms and he instantly set her down. 'Aunt Jude!' Lily called as she hurtled down the hallway, flowers still held tight. 'Guess what I got? You'll never guess…' Her words trailed off and Natasha realised she'd been left alone with Brenton.

'Uh, sorry. Come on in.' As she said the words, a fly buzzed inside as well. Brenton was quick to catch it in his hand and let it go outside before coming in. 'Thanks. I can't stand flies buzzing around the house.'

'I remember,' he said.

Natasha closed the door. 'The flowers were lovely, Brenton. You've made her day.'

'I've always wanted to give lilies to *my* Lily.'

'I remember.' Natasha was glad he was accepting that he

had a daughter. It couldn't possibly be easy for him and a surge of anger shot through her at the meddling his mother had done. She'd robbed them of their life together and, because of it, Brenton had missed out on his daughter's life so far.

'She's certainly a bundle of energy.'

'She doesn't stop.' Natasha laughed as she led the way down the hallway towards the dining room. 'From morning until night, she's just go, go, go.'

'What time does she usually go to bed?'

'Seven-thirty, but as tonight is a special night, we're letting her stay up an extra hour.'

'We?'

'Aunt Jude and I. We need to discuss rules and things like that so we're both consistent when we're with Lily. Children are very good at playing people off against each other.'

'Is that a warning?'

Natasha smiled and shrugged. 'It's an observation, but you could take it as a warning if you like.'

'Don't rock the boat? It's too late for that, Tash.'

'It's not necessarily rocking the boat, Brenton, more of watch the way you climb in. If Lily finds out you're going to be a soft touch, then she'll start to play us off against each other.'

'But she's *six!*'

Natasha raised her eyebrows and nodded. 'Exactly. She's six and most definitely not stupid, which is why we need to be even more careful.' She went to walk into the dining room but he placed a hand on her arm and stopped her.

'Thanks.'

'What for?'

'For telling the truth.'

It took Natasha a moment or two to filter what he was saying as the touch on her arm had sent shock waves of heat and desire through her. As if he'd read her thoughts, he glanced down at his hand before quickly letting go.

He watched the colour suffuse her cheeks and he realised

then how close they were standing. Her perfume wound its way around his senses and the urge to run his hands through her hair, which was still secured in the bun she'd worn to work, almost became too strong to fight.

'I thought I asked you to stop wearing that perfume.'

'Did you? I don't remember.' She leaned against the door-frame, her gaze flicking from his mouth to his eyes.

'You like driving me crazy, don't you?' he whispered, his voice threaded with mounting desire.

'I'm sure the feeling's mutual.'

'Here we go,' Aunt Jude said, as she carried the vase full of lilies towards them. Natasha moved into the dining room whilst Brenton stepped back to allow her aunt to enter.

'They have to go on the table where we can all see them while we're having dinner,' Lily announced, coming to slip her hand into Brenton's. He looked down, slightly startled by the gesture, and Natasha smiled, glad the electric mood between them had been broken.

Lily kept up a steady chatter throughout the meal, telling Brenton the most insignificant details about things, but it was all part of being a parent and Natasha knew, instinctively, that he was lapping it up like a thirsty man in the desert.

Afterwards, Lily showed him her homework and read her book to him. He was highly impressed and praised her accomplishment, making her beam from ear to ear.

'Ms Schlowski said she's going to test me tomorrow on the next level because I can read this one really good.'

'Really well,' Natasha and Brenton automatically corrected. They looked at each other and smiled.

Lily giggled. 'Really well,' she repeated, as she tugged on Brenton's arm. 'Come and see my room, Dad. It's pink and we still have a few boxes to unpack so I don't have all my toys on my bed yet, but it's really cool.'

He rose from where he'd been sitting and let her lead him away. Natasha sighed as she flopped down onto the lounge. 'Whew!'

'She's a little dynamo tonight.' Aunt Jude chuckled as she picked up her knitting.

'I don't know if she'll calm down long enough to sleep.' Natasha laughed.

'It won't hurt to take her to school at recess tomorrow—that way she can have a sleep in,' Aunt Jude added.

'We'll see how she is in the morning.' It *was* an exciting time for Lily and Natasha was determined her daughter should enjoy it. The click-clacking sound of Aunt Jude's knitting needles filled the comfortable silence and they both heard Lily's giggle coming from her room.

'He's certainly stolen *her* heart,' Aunt Jude commented. 'What about yours?'

Natasha frowned. 'Hmm.'

'Too early for judgement? Good girl. I don't want you to be hurt again.'

'And this is Mummy's room,' Natasha heard Lily say, and a moment later she heard the sound of her bedroom door open. With a burst of energy, Natasha was up and out of the chair like a shot. Brenton was still standing in the hallway whilst Lily had obviously gone into the room. She hurried towards them.

'It looks very nice,' he said.

'Here it is,' Lily said, and as Natasha came to stand beside Brenton, she saw her daughter lifting the silver-framed photograph of Brenton from the underwear drawer, a pair of pink lacy knickers falling to the floor.

Natasha was horrified and Lily, seeing the look in her mother's eyes, was instantly contrite. 'Sorry, Mummy, but I just wanted to show Daddy his picture because I don't have one.'

Natasha brushed passed Brenton, ignoring the instant heat that flooded through her at the contact, and snatched the photo from Lily's hands. She picked up her underwear and shoved them both back in the drawer. 'Out,' she said firmly. She risked a glance at Brenton and, where she'd been expecting to find humour, she found empathy. She looked away, slightly puzzled.

'How about,' he said after an uncomfortable pause, placing one hand on Lily's shoulder and gently steering her back up the hallway, 'we each have a picture taken and then you can have your very own one of me and I can have my very own one of you?'

Lily's eyes brightened with happiness. 'That's a great idea, Dad, and then we can have one of you and me and Mummy and Aunt Jude because we're a family. Hey, Aunt Jude, guess what?' Lily ran into the room to tell Aunt Jude the news.

'It's time for you to start getting ready for bed,' Natasha said softly, when Lily had calmed down.

'Aw, Mum. That's not fair. You said I could stay up late.'

'And you have. Look at the clock, Lil.' Natasha pointed to the clock on the wall. Lily looked and then stamped her foot in frustration. She was over-excited now and definitely tired. 'How about if you get ready for bed, then ask Daddy if he'd like to read you some stories?'

The smile was back on Lily's face as she slipped her hands into Brenton's. 'Will you, Daddy? Will you stay and read me some stories?'

'Of course.'

'Yippee.' She bounced up and down.

'Get ready for bed first,' Natasha instructed in her no-non-sense-mother tone.

'OK. And Daddy can check my teeth and put my hair up, too.'

'Go.'

Once Lily had left the room, Brenton turned to her. 'Do I really have to put her hair up?'

Natasha smiled. 'Do you know how?'

'Wouldn't have a clue.'

She laughed and the sound cascaded over him. In that brief moment he relived so many other memories of when she had laughed in that same carefree way. She was more beautiful than she'd been seven years ago, if that was at all possible.

and seeing her here tonight, with Lily, it had shown him that she was a good mother. A man couldn't ask for more as far as his child was concerned. *His* child! He still couldn't believe it.

When Lily returned, he felt self-conscious checking her teeth in front of both Natasha and Jude but check them he did. When Lily handed him the hairbrush, he ummed and ahhed. It was obvious Natasha wasn't going to help him out with this one, and he knew without looking at her that she was enjoying his discomfort.

'You know, Lily, I haven't had much practice at putting up six-year-old girls' hair.'

'I'm almost seven,' she protested hotly.

'I'm sorry. Almost seven-year-old girl's hair. How about if your mummy does it tonight so I can watch? After all, I wouldn't want to hurt you.'

'Come here,' Natasha said on a laugh, deciding to give in and take over before Lily made a scene. 'The sooner your hair is done, the sooner Daddy can read you some books.'

'Why do you need to have it up?' he asked as he watched Natasha expertly pull the auburn tresses up into a high ponytail.

'Because I have eczema and I sweat at night-time if my hair is down. That's why I have the shiny slippery satin pillowcase I showed you.' Lily's words were said very matter-of-factly.

'You have eczema?' Brenton turned to look at Natasha who nodded.

'It's not too bad. It was worse when she was a baby but she's on soy products and needs to watch what she eats. All right, missy, you're all done. Give Aunt Jude and I a kiss and then Daddy can take you to bed.'

'Yippee.' Lily started bounding around excitedly again. She did as she was told and ran off to find some story books.

'So what's the protocol?' Brenton asked a little nervously.

'Three stories, prayers and then there's a CD player by her bed which you need to switch on. She has a night-light by her bed but Lily knows the routine. Just ask her if you're not sure.'

'Daddy!' Lily called from her room in a sing-song voice. 'I'm ready!'

'Enjoy it,' Natasha said softly, as Brenton headed out of the room.

When he walked into Lily's room, he found it lit by a bedside lamp and she had three story books sitting on the edge of her bed. 'So, where do I sit?'

'Well, Aunt Jude sits in the middle but Mummy usually sits up here right beside me and puts her legs up on the bed and puts her arm around me so I can snuggle in.'

'Oh. Well…er…what would you like me to do?'

Lily thought for a moment. 'Do it the way Mummy does because, you know, you're my dad!'

'Good idea,' he said with a smile. She moved over and he sat back, leaning against the headboard. She snuggled beneath his arm as he opened the first story book. The feel of her head against his chest, the smallness of her body close to his made his heart fill with love. This child had accepted him unconditionally and he'd never had that before. Correction—he'd only had that once before, and that had been with Lily's mother.

He started to read, deciding to simply enjoy this experience. When he'd finished the first story, Lily showed him how to dim her bedside light. 'Mummy does it when she's finished reading the third book and…' big yawn '…I'm feeling really sleepy so I thought I'd better tell you now.'

'Thank you, Lily.' She snuggled back into his arms and kissed the top of her head.

'Daddy?'

The question was soft. 'Yes?'

'Promise me you'll look after Mummy and me for ever and never go away again.'

Brenton's heart constricted with love and it was then he truly realised he would be in Natasha's life for ever. Lily was their common denominator and, although he'd been telling himself over and over again that it was wrong to get involved with Natasha, he knew he was fighting a losing battle. Lily would unite them for ever and regardless of whether he still thought of Natasha as a lying, cheating woman—as his mother had portrayed—or not, the fact remained that Lily was *their* child.

'Promise me, Daddy.' Lily's voice was filled with concern now and she shifted to look up at him. The depths of her blue eyes radiated uncertainty and Brenton knew he could never leave her, even if he wanted to.

'I promise, Lily,' he said softly. She reached up and kissed his cheek, the uncertainty disappearing in a flash before she snuggled back down into his arms. Halfway through the book, he realised her breathing had deepened and she'd become heavier in his arms. He paused and said softly, 'Lily?' No answer. Now what? Should he stay here? Could he move her? If he did, would she wake? Slowly he closed the book—no protest. He shifted slightly off the bed—no protest. He gently moved her from his arms and laid her head on her satin pillow—no protest. The only sound she made was a small sighing noise before her breathing settled into a steady rhythm. He stretched his arms before dimming her light and switching the music on.

He stood, looking down at the small figure in the bed, and shook his head in disbelief.

'Well done,' Natasha said softly, coming into the room. She stood beside him and it seemed the most natural thing in the world for him to put his arm about her shoulders. She tensed momentarily but then relaxed and leaned into him a little.

'She's…amazing, Tash.'

Natasha smiled. 'That she is.'

'She's so…you.'

Natasha looked up at him. 'She's both of us,' she whispered. Brenton turned his head and gazed into her eyes. Neither of them spoke—not with words. Slowly, ever so slowly, Brenton leaned down and brushed his lips across hers.

The touch was feather-light and ended almost as soon as it had begun.

It hadn't been a romantic kiss but more an acknowledgement of what they shared—Lily.

As he watched Lily, Natasha watched him. Even in the dimly lit room, she was amazed at how little he'd changed. His face was the same as her memory recalled, except for a few extra wrinkles—or laughter lines, as she preferred to call them—at the corners of his eyes. His nose was slightly crooked due to a break, thanks to his rugby buddies, and his hair was slightly shorter than she recalled. All in all, though, he was still Brenton and he still affected her in exactly the same way.

After taking a few deep breaths, she shifted her weight, glad to find her knees were now co-operating. She moved out of his embrace but took his hand in hers. 'Come on,' she whispered, and led him from the room. Once outside, in the bright artificial lighting, the spell was broken and he let go of her hand. What had she expected?

They headed back to the lounge room where Aunt Jude was still knitting. 'Asleep?' she asked.

'Snoring peacefully.'

'She doesn't snore. I'm sure of that,' Brenton remarked.

'Don't you believe it,' Aunt Jude stated. She laid her knitting down and stood. 'Tea or coffee?' she asked Brenton.

'Tea, thank you.' At his reply, Aunt Jude left them alone. Natasha knew it was a strategic retreat on her aunt's part but felt herself growing nervous again. She massaged her temples as she sat down. It was all too complicated.

'Headache?' Brenton sat beside her. She shifted closer to the edge of the lounge, putting a bit more distance between them.

'Constantly.'

'For how long?' His tone was authoritative—his 'doctor' voice.

'Since I first saw you on Monday,' she replied with a sigh. 'Brenton, you've got to understand this has been a big upheaval in my life. I grieved for you for many years and in some ways still do—uh, did—but I've managed to pull my life together and go on.'

'For Lily's sake?'

'For her sake, for my sake.' She shrugged. 'There was nothing else to do but to go on.'

'You married another man.'

She turned to look at him. His words held a slight accusatory edge and she wondered whether his feelings ran deeper than she'd initially presumed. 'I was told you were dead, Brenton. I was shown a death certificate. My husband had died. I *had* to get on with my life. It wouldn't have been healthy to always be looking back, to live in the past. Yes, I married again but he knew the truth. He knew and accepted that he wasn't my one true love. He was a good man and he cared about Lily and me.' She made sure she didn't raise her voice but the thread of anger he'd stirred within her was becoming harder to control.

'You married him for convenience.'

'Don't judge me.' Natasha snapped as she turned to face him. 'Don't you dare judge me or my motives. I may have married again for…different reasons, but marrying for love had caused me the most brutal pain ever and I didn't want to go through that again.'

'What, you weren't hurt when he died?'

Natasha slapped his face, hot, angry tears blurring her vision. Brenton stared at her in shock and surprise. Unable to bear his gaze any longer, she stood and walked over to the window, the tears streaming quietly down her face, her shoulders shaking slightly.

It felt like an eternity—standing there, her hands covering her face, trying to control the emotions coursing through her, all the while wondering what he might do or say next.

'Tash.' He'd moved. She hadn't heard him and his nearness startled her, although she refused to turn around. He placed his hands on her bare arms. 'I'm sorry.' He urged her to turn and as she felt so emotionally drained she allowed him the control. Gently he prised her hands from her face and lifted her chin so their gazes could meet.

He looked into her eyes and was sorry for the pain she felt but not for what he'd said. His mother had warned him, years ago, that if he ever met Natasha again, she'd blame him for everything. The thought of her in another man's arms—regardless of the circumstances—filled him with pure jealousy.

He wiped the tears from her eyes and kissed her forehead, then her cheeks. Her eyelids fluttered closed as she sniffed and hiccuped. She didn't want to feel like this. Her stomach was churned up with nervousness and anticipation; her heart ached and her head hurt. Her breathing was still catching slightly in the back of her throat, her lips trembling with need.

Oh, if only he would hold her close, kiss her soundly and tell her everything would be all right. The attraction between them was still as strong as ever but so much had happened. Had too much water passed under the bridge?

He kissed the tip of her nose and she knew the next place his mouth would settle would be on her lips. She opened her eyes, wanting it with one breath and not with the next. If he kissed her now, what would it mean? Where would it take them?

He saw her hesitation. Even though he wanted to crush her to him and plunder her mouth, he realised it was all moving way too fast—and not only for her. He still had many unanswered questions. Right now was not the time to start something up with Natasha and, after taking a steadying breath, he forced himself to step away.

He raked a hand through his hair and shook his head. 'I can't get within a metre of you without wanting to grab you and kiss you senseless, Tash.' His smile was crooked. Her heart turned over again. 'We both know there are so many things to talk about and get to the bottom of, but in all seriousness our first priority should be Lily. Come and sit back down so we can talk.'

Natasha found she couldn't move. She wanted to but her brain was still sluggish from his close proximity. 'Why did you say that?' she asked in a whisper. 'You never used to say hateful or spiteful things like that.'

He nodded, not even pretending he didn't know what she was talking about. 'It was…insensitive of me, Tash. I know you would have grieved for him.' He shrugged his shoulders. 'I guess we've both changed a lot.' He rubbed his cheek where she'd slapped him and she looked away.

'I'm not going to apologise for that, Brenton.'

'I don't expect you to. I deserved it.' She met his gaze again, surprised at his words. Jude came back in carrying a tea-tray, which she placed on the coffee-table. She looked at Brenton and then Natasha.

'Perhaps I should leave you alone for a bit longer.' Without waiting for a reply from either of them, Jude picked up her knitting and hurried from the room.

'Subtle,' he remarked.

'As a sledgehammer.' She reached forward and took her cup of tea. 'So, you want to discuss Lily?'

'Yes.' Brenton poured milk into his tea and stirred it. 'I'm impressed, Tash. She's a well-adjusted, bright little girl. You should be proud of yourself.'

'I'm proud of her.' She sipped her tea.

'I would really like to see a lot more of her.'

'I'm positive the feeling is mutual. I'm sure we could work out an arrangement, you know, depending on our schedules. Like when I'm rostered on over a weekend, she can stay with you.'

'Careful, Tash. Don't forget I'm the one who draws the rosters up,' he said with a mischievous grin.

'I'm sure you'd be fair,' she replied with a smile. 'You'd better be.'

'Do you think it might be disruptive to Lily? You know, sleeping over at my house?'

As he said the words out loud, something awful started tugging at Natasha's heart. He would be spending time with Lily—alone. She had always been there for Lily. *Always*. Now Brenton was here and could take over some of the parenting responsibilities. The only problem was, Natasha wasn't so sure she could let go.

She chose her words carefully. 'I'm sure Lily would be delighted to have a sleepover at your house but we need to remember that this is all very new to her. You're like a shiny new toy and that means she'll push her boundaries and perhaps even play us off against each other.'

'I understand, but we're just going to have to muddle through as best we can.'

'Until we moved in with Aunt Jude, it's basically been Lily and me for her whole life. I'm the one who's been responsible for her. Now…now I have to share her with you, and although I'm more than happy to do that,' she rushed on quickly in case he got the wrong idea, 'I also know it isn't going to be easy.'

He took her free hand in his. 'We'll get there, Tash. Somehow, we'll get there.' Brenton finished his tea, knowing it was time to leave the household in peace. He was glad she was living with Jude and not having to cope all by herself any more.

She walked him to the door and after a brief moment of awkwardness he gave her shoulder a little squeeze before turning and striding to his car. He headed home, his thoughts coming hard and fast on top of one another and, like pieces of a puzzle, he started sorting them into a logical pattern.

He wanted to be with Lily, spend time with her, get to know her, but he also appreciated Natasha's concerns. This was a big upheaval in Lily's life and they needed to find the best solution so the upheaval wasn't prolonged.

When he got home, he walked through his apartment, trying to imagine Lily here. He'd have to change a few things—cleaning out the spare room would be top of the list. He'd need to buy her bedroom furniture among other things.

He shook his head. She wasn't going to cope well with this change. Sure, temporarily it might suit but not in the longer term. He headed to the kitchen and switched the kettle on. It wasn't only Lily he wanted to see more of, he realised

Natasha was becoming every bit as important to him as she had in the past.

Lily was his daughter. One look at her and he was positive of that fact. So why had his mother told him Natasha was pregnant by another man? It didn't add up. He left the kitchen and went into his study, walking purposefully towards the safe beneath his desk.

After twirling the combination, he opened the heavy door and pulled out a folder which contained his official documents. He sorted through them until he came to the one he wanted—his divorce decree.

Slowly, he opened it up. There, where it should be, was Natasha's signature. It was stamped in all the right places and appeared to be legitimate. If it was a forged document, why would his mother go to so much trouble?

He knew she'd never approved of Natasha but he'd always hoped that at some point his mother might come to see Natasha as he'd seen her—the woman who'd accepted him for who he was, not for what his surname was or how much money he had.

Something wasn't right and he determined to call his solicitor, an old friend from school, first thing in the morning and have him check out the paper in front of him. He needed to get to the bottom of things.

CHAPTER SEVEN

THURSDAY was a relatively quiet day as far as A & E went, with just the usual complaints. Brenton sought Natasha out after lunch, finding her sitting down in the tearoom, her head leaning against the wall, her eyes closed, a cup of tea on the table in front of her.

'Relaxed?'

Her eyes snapped open to look at him and she sat up. 'Tired.'

'Still not sleeping well?' He pulled up a chair and sat down next to her.

She smiled wryly. 'It's getting better.'

He nodded. 'Listen, I won't keep you long but I was wondering if I could invite myself around for dinner again this evening.'

'Sure. Aunt Jude always makes too much anyway, but I'll give her a call to let her know.'

'You don't mind?'

'Of course not. I understand you want to see Lily.'

He smiled and shook his head in wonder. 'She's amazing.'

'Yes.'

He leaned forward a little and said in a conspiratorial whisper, 'I think she gets it from me.'

Natasha laughed. 'You always had a giant-sized ego.' She drained her teacup and stood. 'I'd better get back to it.'

He stood slowly and nodded. 'Of course.'

The atmosphere changed from one of joviality to sensuality instantly. Natasha's eyes closed for a second as she tried to control her wayward thoughts, trying to draw on strength from somewhere—anywhere.

'We'll get there,' he murmured, and her eyes snapped open.

She swallowed and he stepped back. 'See you tonight.' He turned and walked from the room, wondering how much longer he'd be able to control himself.

The rest of the day passed quickly and dinner was an even more enjoyable event than the previous night as everyone was more relaxed.

'Not staying?' Natasha asked once Lily was settled in bed.

'Not tonight.' He smiled. 'I need to get some work done.'

She nodded. 'Would you like to come around for dinner tomorrow night?'

'That would be lovely.'

'In fact, I'm sure Aunt Jude wouldn't mind if we made it a regular thing. That way you at least to get see Lily every day.'

'It's a start. All right, I accept.'

'Good.' She walked him to the door and, just as he'd done the previous night, he gave her shoulder a little squeeze before heading home.

Walking into his deserted house, he went to his study to check the messages on his answering-machine and sure enough, there was one from his solicitor. He checked his telephone book and dialled his friend's home number.

'Pierce. It's Brenton. You have some news for me?'

'Yes. I've checked over the papers you couriered to me this morning and they're a no-go.'

'Meaning?'

'They're not legal, mate.'

'What?'

'They're not legal.'

'Explain.'

'They were never submitted, never filed.'

'But I had a meeting with my mother's solicitor. I signed all the necessary forms and everything.'

'And this is the same solicitor who signed this divorce?'

'Yes.'

'He was disbarred years ago.'

'What?'

'Yeah, came as a shock to me, too, mate, but there you have it.'

'But…' Brenton tried to get his mind around what he was being told. 'But he'd been the solicitor representing our family for years. My father used to use him in business.'

'Well, this particular solicitor was found guilty on quite a few fraud charges. Regardless of this fact, your divorce papers were never filed.'

'That means—' He broke off and raked his hand through his hair.

'That your marriage is still legal? Yes, it does. I've doubled-checked that for you.'

Brenton breathed in deeply, exhaling slowly. 'I'm still married to Tash?'

'One hundred per cent.'

His mind was racing like a freight train. 'Tash remarried, though.'

'When?'

'Three and a half years ago.'

'Is she still married?'

'Widowed.' There was silence on the other end of the phone. 'Pierce?'

'She would have needed to lodge her copy of the divorce papers and as—'

'No.'

'No, what?'

'She doesn't have divorce papers.' He shook his head, knowing how weird this was going to sound. 'She had a death certificate. At least, that's what she's told me.'

'Death certificate,' Pierce repeated.

'Yes.'

'Can I see it?'

'I'll get it for you.'

'Good.'

'But you're sure my marriage to her is still legal?'

'Absolutely, but I need that death certificate. If she remarried, then she would have committed bigamy.'

'Bigamy?'

'That's right. It's a federal offence.'

Brenton couldn't believe what he was hearing.

'Get me those papers and I'll contact a buddy of mine who specialises in federal law.'

'Right. Thanks, mate. I appreciate your help.' Brenton disconnected the call and sat back in his chair. Natasha was his wife. Natasha was his wife!

He stood up and began to pace the room. This meant everything his mother had told him was a lie. Tash running off with another man, wanting a divorce. It was all lies. He ground his teeth together, unable to believe how he'd let her manipulate his life. Not only his but Natasha's and Lily's as well.

She would have known Natasha was pregnant and because of her deception he'd missed the first six—almost seven years of Lily's life. He thumped the desk in anger but it wasn't enough. Storming out into the living room, he picked up a photograph of his mother, one she'd given him years ago.

He stared down into the face of the woman who had always looked so regal…so dignified…so above reproach.

'Lies,' he snarled, and hurled the picture across the room, feeling a sense of satisfaction when the glass smashed, the frame falling bent and broken to the floor.

Natasha was his wife! This put a whole new angle on things. He was still officially married to her and he intended to do everything he could to make sure they stayed together—for ever.

He was a man who took his wedding vows seriously.

When Natasha arrived at work the next morning, it was to find A & E buzzing with activity—yet all but one of the examination cubicles were empty. Brenton was at the nurses' station, on the phone, frantically scribbling down notes on a piece of paper.

'Oh, good, you're here,' Annie said.

'What's going on?'

'Retrieval. Deb?' She called over one of her nurses. 'Deb, can you show Natasha where the retrieval overalls are and get her ready, please?'

'Sure.'

'What's happened?' Natasha asked as she followed the nurse.

'The King Island ferry has run aground or something like that. Brenton's just getting the final information from the emergency services.' They quickly got changed and headed back to where Brenton was just putting the phone down.

'Listen up, people,' he called. 'The King Island vehicle and passenger ferry has hit some foreign object and has started to take in water. Authorities think a scuttled ship from years ago has shifted, which is what's possibly caused the rupture.

'Its position is just outside Queenscliff with approximately twenty vehicles and about seventy people on board. The official count hasn't been determined yet but they're working on it. The emergency helicopter will be here in ten minutes to take the retrieval team out. All emergency crews will participate and if the medical need is too great, we'll be calling in Melbourne. For now we're the closest hospital so we'll take the majority of priority-one cases. Really bad cases will go straight to Melbourne. Annie, you stay here and monitor from this end. Someone find Paul Jamieson and alert him of the retrieval. I want Brian Newton and his orthopaedic registrars standing by to receive casualties as they arrive.'

'Do you want Paul out on retrieval with you?' Annie asked.

'It might be a help. See if you can get him here in the next nine minutes, otherwise we'll cope.' His gaze drifted over Natasha as he spoke. 'That's it. Let's get moving.'

As Natasha wasn't sure where the equipment was kept, she waited for someone to give her directions. Brenton walked up and, standing rather close, said in an intimate whisper, 'You look rather sexy in those bright orange overalls but, then, you look sexy in just about anything.'

Natasha's jaw hung open and she could feel herself blushing. Before she had time to reply, he'd walked off. What had got into him this morning?

'Natasha? Can you give us a hand?' someone called, and she headed over to help.

When they arrived at the scene, the police boat took them out to the grounded ferry. She mentally went through a number of different scenarios of what they might find.

'Most of the uninjured foot passengers are being evacuated now, but some people are trapped in their vehicles below,' the police rescue officer informed them.

'How many paramedics are currently on board?' Brenton asked.

The police officer checked his information sheet. 'Six. They're doing a sweep and rendering first aid, as well as grading people as to their medical priority. We need to work fast because there's a southerly front on the way and we have just over two hours before it hits. The bureau predicts a swell of between two and three metres.'

'Right.' Brenton split the six of them up into teams. 'And, Tash, you go with Deb,' he said finally. Three doctors and three nurses. Thankfully, Paul had just come out of Theatre a few minutes before the retrieval team had left. 'The helicopter is standing by for priority-one cases. Give clear instructions whether the patient is to go to Melbourne or Geelong Hospital,' he continued. 'Triage and stabilise. Other patients will be transported to Geelong via road. Lifejackets are to be worn at all times. I don't care how cumbersome they are, we'll just have to work around them.'

The police boat pulled carefully alongside the ferry and one by one they were helped aboard. The police officer in charge on the ferry gave them walkie-talkies and directions. 'We've moved those that we could into one area up top.' He pointed up the stairwell. 'We have five cases to the left and down those steps and two to the right around there.'

'Paul, you go to the right. Tash, you and I will go this way,' Brenton said, and they all moved off.

'Over here,' they heard a voice call once they'd descended

the stairwell. Tash looked over and saw a paramedic crouch
ing beside a supine body.

'I'll take this one,' she said to Brenton. He nodded an
moved on. She crouched down with Deb. 'Status?' She pulle
on a pair of gloves and reached for her medical torch, check
ing the patient's pupils as she listened to the paramedic.

'He fell over the handrail up there and hit his head on th
rail down here when he landed.' Natasha looked up. The ma
had fallen a good three metres. 'Regained consciousness abou
fifteen minutes ago and was given morphine. Right leg feel
fractured and neurovascular pulse in right ankle is thready.'

'Set up an IV,' she said to Deb as she took out her stetho
scope and listened to the man's chest, heart and lungs. Sh
felt his skull but found only a bump. 'Skin's not broken.' Nex
she checked his right leg. 'Fractured tibia and fibula, left ankl
feels sprained. Can you hear me?' she called, but received n
response. 'Splint his leg, put a neck brace on him and he ca
be moved. Monitor for concussion but the fact that he's re
gained consciousness and received analgesics is a good sig
Priority two.' She took out a pen and wrote something on th
man's tag before picking up her bag. 'Where's the next per
son?'

'Around the corner as far as I know.'

'Catch up when you're done, Deb,' Natasha said, befor
heading off. She saw the next patient with a police offic
kneeling beside him.

'I've only just found him,' the officer said. 'I was just goin
to call it in.'

Natasha put her bag down and changed her gloves befor
starting the examination. 'Can you hear me?' she calle
loudly, and received a murmured response. The man was ly
ing on his stomach, one hand outstretched as though he'
been trying to pull himself along. Slowly she turned him ove
and checked the man's pupils. 'Do you remember what hap
pened?'

'Fell,' he mumbled.

'Not to worry.' She listened to his chest, heart and lung

'Everything seems fine. Where does it hurt?' She checked his bones but couldn't feel any breaks.

'Stomach.'

She handed the police officer the portable sphygmomanometer. 'Take his blood pressure. Are you allergic to anything?' she asked as she moved his clothes out of the way so she could palpate his abdomen.

'No.' He groaned when she pressed on the right side of his abdomen.

'Have you had your appendix out?'

'No.'

'Can you remember what happened? Did you fall onto something?' She continued checking.

'Crashed into a railing and then fell down.'

'BP is 120 over 50.'

'I'm going to give you something for the pain which should help.' Natasha drew up the shot as Deb came around the corner. 'Call for Paul on the walkie-talkie and have him check this patient out. Abdominal pain, intense on the lower right-hand side.'

'Appendix?'

'Possibly.' She looked at the police officer. 'Do you have any of those tags?' He nodded and she gave him instructions as to what to put on this patient's tag.

'Tash?' She heard Brenton's shout. 'Tash, are you near?'

'Why did they give us walkie-talkies?' Deb mumbled.

'Tash?'

'Go,' Deb said. 'I'll finish up here.'

'Brenton?' she called as she headed in the direction of his voice. She rounded another corner but couldn't find him. 'Brenton?'

'Down here,' he said, and she looked over the side of the rail to the next level of the ferry. It was where some of the vehicles were parked.

'How do I get down there?'

'Keep going around and you'll find a staircase. Hurry.'

Natasha followed his directions and made her way through

the maze of cars, some having crashed into each other on impact. The upper half of Brenton's body was inside a car, the nurse working with him handing him the instruments he needed. The driver's side of the car had smashed into the ferry wall, crushing the front half of the car.

'Careful, the deck's uneven,' he warned. 'We were walking by and heard these muffled cries for help. Sixteen-year-old girl—Meg is her name. She's slipping in and out of consciousness, BP is low. Pupils equal and reacting to light. Hand me a neck brace. We need to get her out of the car so I can assess her injuries properly. Her legs seem to be wedged. Not sure whether it's the steering column or something else.'

Natasha bent down, trying to gauge her angles. 'Let me see if I can get through. Shift to the side a bit, Brenton.' As she spoke, she took off her lifejacket. When Brenton glared at her she shrugged. 'I won't fit otherwise.' Before he could say another word, she slithered along the floor of the car and felt it shift. 'Whoa!'

'Tash what are you doing?' he demanded hotly.

'Check the handbrake. Is it on?'

She waited.

'No.' Then she heard the sound of him applying the brake.

'I'm going to move again,' she said, and reached out to pull herself forward. 'OK. I can see her legs now. Hold on, Meg. We'll have you out of here in no time.' She shifted a bit further. 'Brenton, her right foot is jammed beneath the pedal. There's quite a bit of blood. I'll need some scissors and a bandage for a tourniquet. Also see if you can get me a saw or something so I can get the pedal off. Once we have her out, she'll require immediate surgery.'

Natasha started getting hot as she lay on the floor of the car in her retrieval suit. She cut away Meg's thin cotton trousers and most of her strappy sandal. 'Most of the toes on her right foot are crushed. She's going to need to go to Melbourne to see a microspecialist.'

'I'm on it,' Brenton replied.

With only limited area to move, the job of stemming the blood flow was made more complicated.

'How's her BP?'

'Holding. IV is doing the trick and she's had morphine.'

'Good.' She finished applying the tourniquet and started work on the toes, applying a bandage as best she could. 'Any news on that saw?'

'It's on its way.'

'Good.' She shifted forward a little more, then winced in pain. 'Aagh!'

'Tash? Tash, what is it?'

She clenched her teeth hard together. 'I've…pulled a muscle,' she muttered.

'What?'

'I've pulled a muscle,' she said more loudly. 'It's all right.' It wasn't. She was in a lot of pain. It seemed to stretch from the middle of her back right up to one shoulder. 'Have you got that saw?'

'Yes.'

She tried to turn slightly so she could grasp it with her pain-free hand. 'Slide it down the seat a little more, Brenton.' He did as she asked and she finally grasped it. Carefully, she brought it up to her other hand, ensuring the blades didn't catch on anything. Finally, she had it in place and, straining hard with every move she made, she started to cut through the pedal. It seemed to take for ever and she had to stop every now and then to rest.

'Come on, Tash. You can do it,' Brenton encouraged.

After what seemed to be an eternity, she was able to move the pedal enough to gently slide Meg's foot out of the way. 'OK. It's free.' She collapsed in a heap, overcome by the pain running down her right-hand side.

'Can you move?' His voice was soothing.

'I don't know.'

'Which muscle?'

His question immediately took her back to the time when they would play the 'what are you wearing' game on the phone. 'Latissimus dorsi and probably infraspinatus,' she replied with a weary smile.

'Ouch. Come on, Tash. Let's get you out.'

'Meg?'

'We can't move her until you're out of the way.'

Taking a deep breath, she passed him the saw and other instruments before slowly wriggling backwards.

'Easy, easy.'

Every movement hurt and she was cross with herself for not having been more careful in the first place. She groaned.

'It was an accident,' he said softly, staring down into her pain-ridden face.

'What are you? A mind-reader?' Slowly she emerged from the car, Brenton's hands gently guiding her. She collapsed to the deck.

'Don't move,' he ordered her.

'Couldn't if I wanted to.'

With the help of Deb and one of the paramedics, they were able to manoeuvre Meg from the front seat of the car. She was strapped securely into a stretcher and taken away. Brenton knelt down beside Natasha.

'How are you holding up?'

'I've had better days.'

'Let me take a look.'

'It's all right. I'll be fine.' She waved his concern away.

'Natasha.' She opened her eyes wide at the use of her full name. 'You're being stubborn.'

'We've got more patients to see.'

'No, actually, we don't. The vessel has been swept from top to toe during the last hour.'

'Hour?'

'Yes, Tash. I guess time flies when you're having fun.'

She smiled at his attempt at humour. 'All right. You can have a look but not here. Let's get on up to a higher level.'

'Agreed.' He helped her to her feet, picked up her lifejacket and collected their medi-kits. She tried not to wince with every step but any movement at the moment was causing her discomfort. 'Hurt to breathe?'

'A little.'

'Liar.' He smiled at her. 'I know you too well, remember.'

When they were up another level, he said, 'Right. Off with your retrieval suit and let me take a look.' She didn't protest, knowing it was futile. She closed her eyes, trying not to focus on the fact that Brenton was about to look at her body. It was ridiculous. He'd seen her naked a thousand times before but this…was different.

Slowly, she pulled the zipper down on her suit and together they gently peeled the material down until her right arm and side were exposed. She wore only her white cotton bra beneath and immediately felt completely vulnerable.

'No wonder it's sore,' he murmured. 'Not only have you pulled the muscles, you've grazed yourself.' In another minute he'd squeezed some antiseptic cream onto his hands and was rubbing it tenderly over her skin. Natasha closed her eyes, willing herself to regain some kind of control over her wayward emotions, but it was no good.

Just the simple touch of his hand on her body was enough to heat her blood, increase her heartbeat and make her knees go weak. She stumbled forward, trying to keep her balance. Why did her head feel dizzy all of a sudden? She breathed in, trying desperately to slow her pulse rate down, but all she succeeded in doing was breathing in the scent of him. Brenton. Just the way she remembered.

'There,' he said briskly, his tone thick with desire. 'I think that should do it for now.' He cleared his throat as he helped her put her suit back on. 'You won't be able to use an anti-inflammatory gel on your muscles as your skin is broken, so when we get back to the hospital I'll give you an injection.'

'Thanks,' she said over her shoulder, unable to meet his gaze. She picked up her lifejacket and started putting it back on. Brenton quickly helped her. 'Thanks,' she said again. His walkie-talkie buzzed and he quickly answered it.

'We're heading up right now,' he said and, handing her one of the medi-kits, walked ahead.

He didn't speak another word to her until after they were back at the hospital. He took her into an examination cubicle and gave her an injection of a non-steroidal anti-inflammatory. 'That should help.'

'Thanks.' She was sitting up on the examination bed, buttoning up the cream shirt she'd put on that morning.

'Let me know if the pain persists.'

'I will.' She stood and tucked her shirt into her dark grey skirt. 'Thanks.'

'Tash, I want to move into your aunt's house.'

'What?' Natasha gaped at him. 'What?' She shook her head, not sure she'd heard right.

'I think it will be in everyone's best interest if I move in to your aunt's house.'

'But…but…why?'

'There are a few reasons, most of which I don't want to discuss in an examination cubicle. We can discuss it after dinner tonight.'

'OK,' she sighed.

'Good. I've got meetings so I'll meet you there. We can talk once Lily's in bed.' He nodded and walked out.

Natasha found it increasingly difficult to concentrate for the rest of the day. The anti-inflammatory definitely did the trick but when she went for her afternoon cup of tea she was starting to feel a little worse for wear.

'So what's new?' Annie asked as she sat down opposite Natasha in the cafeteria.

Natasha sighed heavily. 'Brenton wants to move into my aunt's house.'

'You don't look too happy with the idea.'

'I'm just so confused, Annie. Everything is happening at the rate of knots. I'm not sure whether it's a good decision or a bad one.'

Annie smiled reassuringly. 'At least he wants to get to know Lily.'

'I know, I know.' Natasha slumped forward onto the table and closed her eyes, trying not to whimper in pain. She took a deep breath and straightened up again. 'I just want some time to come to terms with everything. I mean, four days ago I thought he was dead and now not only is he alive and kicking but it looks as though we've both been fed a pack of lies. His mother went to such extraordinary lengths to separate us.' Natasha shook her head sadly. 'Was I *so* wrong for him? Was I *so* horrible that she wanted to do everything she possibly could to protect him?'

Annie shrugged. 'I:…um…I'm not—'

'I'm not looking for answers, well, not from you,' Natasha clarified with a small smile. 'I'm just stating these questions out loud. You know, we all think we're nice people and we want other people to like us, to be friends with us, to *approve* of us so when someone doesn't—even though it's years ago and the woman in question isn't even alive any more—when you discover someone obviously…*hated* you…' Natasha sighed heavily, trying to control her emotions. 'I tell you, Annie, it makes you feel as though you have some terminal illness. You're plagued. If one person doesn't like you, then how many more will feel the same way? It makes you question yourself. Am I really bad? Did she see something deep inside me I never saw? Have I affected other people? My daughter? Am I instilling bad things into her? Is she going to grow up and have people treat her as I've been treated?' Natasha angrily brushed away an errant tear.

Annie reached across and took Natasha's hand in hers. 'You can't let her win. I had the misfortune to meet Mrs Worthington and, believe me, she made me feel as though I were a bug to be crushed, even though I come from a wealthy family. I went to school with Monty—well, he went to the boys' school and I went to the girls' school, but we had mixers and met after school and all that stuff. We were friends, we still are.'

'So why didn't she approve of you?'

Annie shrugged. 'Wasn't pretty enough? Wasn't charming

enough? Who knows? But more importantly…' she squeezed Natasha's hand '…who cares? *Who* cares? She was just one woman, Natasha, and if you keep on thinking the way you have been, she's still winning.'

Natasha nodded, her lips pursed tightly. 'You're right.' She nodded again. 'You're so right.'

'Don't give her the satisfaction. Don't give her the satisfaction of not working things out with Brenton. You two belong together. You belong with your daughter—as a family.'

'I don't know.' She rubbed a hand across her eyes. 'I'm just so confused about everything that's happened that I don't know any more.'

'*What* don't you know?'

'A lot of things.' Natasha's beeper sounded. She checked the number but didn't move. 'I know I can't keep Brenton from Lily and I don't want to but…well, it's always been the two of us. Just me and Lil, for her whole life. Sure, we've had people come and go from our lives but—'

'You've always had each other,' Annie interrupted.

'I know it's right for Brenton to want to spend time with her and I'm glad he does, I really am.' Natasha smiled involuntarily. 'You should have seen Lily with him. She was so excited and happy. I can't remember a time when she's been this happy.' She looked off into the distance, the smile disappearing slowly.

'Does that bother you?'

'What?'

'That you can't remember a time when she was this happy?'

'Inadequacy?' Annie nodded at her question. 'A bit. It's like all her dreams have come true. She has a mum and she has a dad. Her *real* dad, not just someone I've married.' She sighed wistfully. 'I guess that is enough to make her happy.'

'That's right, and *you're* involved in this equation, too, Natasha. She needs her mum—now more than ever. You're her constant, Natasha.' Annie paused for a moment. 'What about your family? Do you have any siblings?'

Natasha looked down into her empty coffee-cup. 'No.'

'Are your parents alive?' Annie asked the question very softly.

'Yes.'

'I take it you don't see them.'

'No.'

'So you just have your aunt?'

'That's right.'

'Where was your aunt when Mrs Worthington told her pack of lies? Wouldn't she have been able to help shed some light on the situation? I mean, when Brenton returned from overseas.'

'If Aunt Jude had been living in Melbourne then, I doubt whether any of this would have happened. As it was, she was travelling. She didn't have the happiest of childhoods either and just after Brenton and I got married, she set off backpacking around the world. We'd receive the odd postcard now and then but it wasn't until about…four months, I think, after I was told of Brenton's death that I managed to get in contact with Aunt Jude. She'd been living in the mountains in Nepal.' Natasha's pager sounded again and this time she stood up. 'I'd better go. Thanks for the chat. It's helped.'

'Any time,' Annie said with a smile.

As Natasha walked down the corridor towards A & E, she mentally pushed all thoughts of her parents, Brenton and their situation into the dark recesses of her mind. They had no place here at work and her patients deserved one hundred per cent of her attention.

CHAPTER EIGHT

THE first thing Natasha heard when she entered the house was masculine laughter. Her headache instantly increased. She headed to her bedroom, managing to make it without meeting anyone, and closed the door firmly behind her.

She heard Lily squeal with laughter before footsteps bounded down the hallway with heavy masculine ones in pursuit. What was Brenton doing? She dumped her briefcase onto the floor and carefully changed into a blue, sleeveless summer top and a pair of shorts the same colour. She'd just finished pulling them on when her bedroom door was flung open and Lily rushed in, still squealing with laughter.

'Save me, Mummy. Save me.' She giggled and threw herself at Natasha.

Natasha winced in pain. Brenton came over to try and lift Lily from her but Lily obviously thought her father was still playing and pushed her mother backwards onto the bed, just at the moment Brenton lunged.

All three of them ended up sprawled out, Brenton and Natasha's legs twined together with Lily sandwiched between them. The feel of his bare legs against hers was a momentary thrill before the pain of the day's activities made themselves known.

'Ow,' she groaned involuntarily.

Brenton lifted Lily off and it took a moment for the little girl to realise this wasn't a game any more.

'You OK, Tash?'

'Yes.'

'What's wrong, Mummy?'

'Mummy hurt herself at work this morning,' Brenton supplied. 'She'll be all right but we've just got to be careful.'

'Where did you hurt yourself?' Lily wanted to know.

Natasha sat up, her gaze meeting Brenton's, and the scene where he'd rubbed the cream onto her graze replayed itself in her mind. She realised his thoughts were obviously in the same place as his blue eyes, clouded with repressed desire, and she shuddered with longing.

'Down my side, here.' Natasha tenderly lifted her right arm and indicated where it was painful. In the next instant Lily had leaned forward and pressed a kiss on the area. Natasha winced again.

'There you go, Mum. All better.'

She smiled. 'Thanks, honey. So, how was school today?' she asked in a bid to move the subject away from herself.

'Good. We did drama and music today. Mum, can I learn the guitar?'

'That sounds like a good idea. I used to play the guitar when I went to school,' Brenton said.

'Really?' Lily's eyes were wide with wonder.

'Sure. I might still have my old guitar around somewhere. You could use that.'

'Wow! That would be so cool. Wouldn't that be cool, Mum?'

Natasha glared daggers at Brenton. 'We'll see.'

Lily's delighted expression fell. 'That means no.'

'No. It means we'll see. I'll speak to your teacher and find out more about music lessons.'

'But Daddy said I could. He said he'd let me have his old guitar.' She looked soulfully up at Brenton who smiled reassuringly down at her.

Natasha shook her head. 'Go and help Aunt Jude set the table.'

'But, Mum—'

'Lily.' Natasha's tone brooked no argument.

'Oh, all right.' With a resigned shrug Lily walked from the room as though she were going to her own execution.

Brenton stood up. 'All right. What did I do wrong?'

Natasha stood, too. She wanted to blast him, to give him a

piece of her mind, but she also knew this wasn't going to be easy for any of them. She'd had almost seven years of parenting and Brenton had had a few days. She *had* to cut him some slack and at least he'd acknowledged he'd done something wrong!

She sighed. 'First rule of parenting—*never* say yes unless you're absolutely sure it's the right thing to do.'

'What's wrong with her learning the guitar?'

'Nothing, but right now there are too many unknown variables. When will she have guitar lessons? During school or after school? Will it interfere with her school work? How many nights a week should she practise? Is she going to accept this as a commitment? But, most importantly, should she do something new this term? She only started at the school this week. Personally, I'd like her to have at least one term where she can settle in and really make some friends before she decides on any extra-curricular activities.'

He nodded. 'Give me a more clear-cut example of when to say yes.'

'Why? Don't you want to say no to her?'

Brenton put his hands into his navy shorts pockets. It was then she'd noticed he'd changed out of his usual business suit. She stared at his legs for a moment before her gaze travelled up to his chest. It was clad in a white polo shirt which fitted him...*very* well. She gulped, trying to bring her thoughts back into focus.

She turned away for a moment, trying to get her control back. 'You'll have to say no at some point in time, Brenton, otherwise you'll be the ''good'' parent and I'll be the ''bad'' parent.'

'So?'

'Brenton!' She spun around to face him.

'Sorry.' He grinned sheepishly and her heart did a little flip-flop.

'OK.' She looked down at the floor, trying to concentrate. 'You want an example. Can I watch TV? Actually, that's not a good example.'

'Why not?'

'Because first you have to ascertain that she's finished her homework.'

'If she has?'

'Then the answer would be yes—but she knows the TV goes off at half past four because it's time for her bath. OK, here's one. Can I have a shower?'

'Sure, Tash. Don't let me stop you.' He raised his eyebrows suggestively and she tried not to laugh.

'Not me—I'm giving you an example.'

'An example of you in the shower? Actually, I've been there, seen that, but, well, if you insist.'

'Brenton!'

'Natasha!' He mimicked her tone, grinning like a Cheshire cat.

'I think we should discuss this somewhere other than my bedroom.'

'Why?'

'Brenton,' she warned, placing her hands on her hips.

'All right,' he conceded.

She sighed and angled her head, watching him closely. 'What's got into you?'

'Me? Nothing.'

'You've been acting really strange all day,' she said, thinking back to his earlier comment about her retrieval suit.

'Dinner's ready,' Aunt Jude called out. Brenton stood by her open bedroom door, making a low bow and sweeping his hand across his body.

'After you.'

She frowned, still not quite sure what was going on. 'Thank you—I think,' she muttered as she passed him. She watched as Brenton and Lily interacted as though they'd never been apart. She *was* like him in so many ways—not just her eyes. They shared the same sense of humour, they liked the same things. In short, they were on the same wavelength and it made Natasha a little jealous.

Again Brenton read Lily stories, but this time Natasha sat

on the bed beside her daughter, listening intently to the inflections he put on the words. When he started doing the characters' voices, he had both of them laughing.

'Don't excite her too much,' Natasha warned, and he took the hint, reading the last book sensibly. She watched him carefully, noting the way he pressed a heartfelt kiss to Lily's forehead, the way he ran his finger down her cheek and then tapped the end of her nose. The way Lily smiled, happy and secure in the knowledge that she was loved. Natasha's heart swelled with love for Brenton, simply from the way he treated their daughter.

She knew her love for him had never died but now there were too many variables and she wasn't a woman who liked variables. Sort out the garbage, she instructed herself yet again. She must make the effort tomorrow to hunt for that death certificate. Things had been way too hectic and emotional during the past few days to have given it any more than fleeting consideration.

'Let's continue our talk about me moving in here,' Brenton said as they settled in the lounge room.

'You seem pretty intractable on the matter.'

'I am, but I do want to hear your opinion.'

'Why, thank you,' she replied a little sarcastically.

'Tash. It's not like that.'

'All right, so tell me how it is, then.'

He nodded. 'First of all, I think it would be good for Lily.'

'To have you here.'

'Yes. I've been thinking about things. It might be all right in the beginning to have her just for a weekend here or a week there, but I realised…that's not enough. I want to be her father—a *real* father. One who spends as much time with her as he can.

'I had thought about asking both you and Lily to move into my place but that wouldn't be fair on Jude. Besides, the system you have going here, with Jude able to provide care for Lily whenever you're at work, is a good one. It works.'

His words made sense. 'Any other reasons?'

'You.'

'Me?'

'Yes. We need to sort out what's going on between us, Tash. By me moving in here, we'll be able to spend time together away from the hospital, getting to know each other again.' He reached across and took her hand in his. 'We can do this, Tash. We can be parents to Lily. Together.' His blue gaze radiated his excitement.

'What's got into you?' She tried to pull her hand away but couldn't.

He shrugged. 'I guess it's…Lily.' He squeezed her hand before letting it go. 'I couldn't stop thinking about her last night. She's so amazing. She's so like me.'

'I know.' Natasha rolled her eyes.

'Hey, don't get me wrong. She definitely didn't get those auburn locks from me.'

'Great. I get the hair and you get everything else.'

'Tash?' Brenton watched her carefully. 'This can't be easy for you—sharing Lily like this.'

Natasha was silent for a while, trying to choose her words carefully. 'I can't lie to you, Brenton, and say I'm not a little jealous, but it's not in a bad way. She just…' She shrugged. 'I don't know, treats you differently to me.'

'That's because I'm like a new toy. Wait a few months and then she'll be grumbling about me, too.'

A few months! Even the sound of it was scary. 'She grumbles about me?'

'That's not what I said, or what I meant. All kids grumble about their parents—it's a fact of life.'

'True.'

'Although with us, you used to grumble about my mother while I still get churned up inside when I think of the indifferent way your parents treated you.'

'The "accident".' She nodded.

'Still hurts, huh?'

'Not so much since I've had Lil. Sometimes I think I overcompensate, giving her too much attention because I didn't get any from my parents.'

'You can *never* overcompensate with love and attention.'

'I disagree. Your mother is proof of that.'

'That was misguided love.'

'Misguided!' Natasha frowned, making sure she didn't raise her voice too much. 'Brenton—the woman lied and cheated to break us up. She manipulated us. She…she…robbed you of nearly seven years of Lily's life and you can calmly sit there and call it *misguided?*'

'What she did was wrong and—'

'Don't you dare defend her. Don't you dare make excuses for what she's done to us. You have no idea of the emotional trauma I've suffered.' Natasha put her hands over her eyes for a moment before raising her head to meet his gaze, her words soft but forceful. 'She sat in our apartment and blatantly lied, telling me you were dead. By the time I was released from the hospital, she'd packed up all my belongings and found me accommodation in rural Victoria. I saw a psychologist for years, Brenton.' Natasha shook her head in disgust. 'She ruined that part of my life—*our* lives—so, please, don't sit there and blandly excuse what she did.'

'I wasn't going to excuse what she did, Tash.' He stood up and started to pace. 'I have so many unanswered questions running around inside my head, most of which concern you.'

'What did she tell you about me?' The question was a whisper and she closed her eyes in anguish. She wasn't sure whether or not Brenton wanted to talk about it now, but she desperately needed to know. She felt the need to defend herself but she didn't know where to start until she'd heard all the awful accusations and lies his mother had, no doubt, told.

He stopped pacing for a moment and looked down at her. She wasn't sure whether he was really looking at her—really seeing her—or whether his thoughts had already returned to the past.

'When you weren't answering our phone at home, I called her.' He stated the words without emotion. 'I was worried,

First she told me you were probably studying, but it didn't make sense because I knew your routine and even if you were studying at home, you'd still answer the phone.'

Natasha nodded.

'I tried for a few more days and when I still couldn't get hold of you I called her again. I wanted her to go over to our apartment and check things out. She said she wouldn't set foot in the place but that she'd send her chauffeur and let me know. By then I had only two and a half weeks left to go of the rotation before I could come home. You know, Tash, it was the last thing I had to do to complete my internship. If I left before completing it, it wouldn't be accredited.'

Again Natasha nodded, biting her lower lip.

'She called me back a day later and said she had some bad news. You had been seen—with another man.'

Anger surged forcefully within Natasha and she clenched her teeth together. It was as she'd thought.

'She said she'd spoken to you on the phone, saying that I'd been trying to get in touch, but that you'd merely laughed and hung up. She said she knew the man was there with you because she could hear him in the background.' Brenton raked his hand roughly through his hair and shook his head. 'I didn't want to believe her. I *couldn't* believe you'd do something like that to me.'

Natasha gasped. 'I didn't.' Surely he didn't believe these lies his mother had told him. Unease was added to her anger. 'You know it's a lie, don't you?' She stood and walked over to him. 'Brenton?'

'I didn't know what to believe at the time, Tash.' He shook his head.

'How about the wedding ring you put on my finger?' Her words were said with determination and she held up the ring, which was now on her right hand. 'I haven't been able to take it off, Brenton. It may not be on the correct hand but I have *always* worn it.' She was mad at him now. 'How could you think I would do such a thing to you? Didn't you know me at all?'

Brenton didn't reply. Instead, he turned and looked out into the darkness of the night. 'I didn't want to believe any of it but I had two weeks to stew on this information and no way of contacting you. When I came home and found you were gone—all your belongings, our life together gone—what else was I to believe? The evidence spoke for itself.'

'It wasn't true.' Natasha whispered the words to his back, her voice choked with emotion. 'It wasn't true, B.J. You've *got* to believe me.'

He turned to face her, his expression filled with hurt. 'Why would my mother go to such enormous lengths to keep us apart?'

Natasha frowned, before staring at him in amazement. 'You really don't know?'

'No. Tell me.'

Natasha took a step towards him. 'She'd lost you.' Her heart was pounding double time against her ribs, emotion-filled tears were brimming in her eyes and her lips were red from being bitten. 'She'd lost you,' she stated again. She stood before him and placed her hand tenderly on his cheek.

Brenton closed his eyes for a moment, accepting the tenderness of her touch.

'You were *everything* to her. Now, as a mother, I can kind of understand her motivation, even though it was completely wrong. She'd lost you, Brenton. From the moment you were born, she'd succeeded in providing an heir to your family's fortune. A male Worthington to carry on the line. She would have been like a little girl planning her wedding day as she anticipated all the wonderful things you would do with your life.

'Your father was so immersed in his work that he had no time for her. That was quite evident from the way she spoke of him. So, instead of fussing over him, she turned her attention to you. In doing so, she was trying to show your father that she took her job as wife and mother seriously. High hopes, great expectations, and you lived up to all of them.'

'Except for you,' Brenton whispered.

'Exactly.' Natasha reluctantly withdrew from him, taking a step away. 'I wasn't the woman she'd chosen for you to marry and you'd done the most hurtful thing, in her opinion, that a son could do. You'd turned your back on her advice, on her counsel and on her love. You'd chosen for yourself.'

'But I—'

'It doesn't matter what you thought you were doing—that is how she would have seen it. I look at Lily and all I want for her is the best. The best of absolutely everything. I don't want her to find out how horrible this world can be.' Natasha's lower lip began to tremble. 'I want her to know that I'm always here for her, no matter what, but above all else I want her to be happy.' She nodded. 'Oh, yes, I can understand your mother's initial motivation because I'm now a mother. I cherish Lily.' She squeezed her eyes shut and sniffed. 'She is everything to me.' The words were whispered and it took a moment for Natasha to get her thoughts back on track. 'But there's one thing I've vowed never to do, and that is to control her life.

'Guitar lessons are only a choice, and at this age and for quite a few more years to come she'll need guidance. My aim, as her mother, is to give her good guidance, help her to make her own decisions and to be confident in her opinions as well as herself. Your mother was happy enough for you to make decisions when she'd given her approval, but with me you never once sought her opinion. You met me, you fell in love with me and you married me.'

'But she knew about you. We were friends for years.'

'And I'm sure she was more than happy for us to remain just friends. She probably advised you not to get too serious about me as all I wanted was your money.'

'She said that about everyone at med school. She didn't know you like I did.'

'She didn't want to, Brenton, because I wasn't her choice. In getting rid of me, she was able to get you back again.'

'I went through mental anguish and torment.' He turned and walked away from her, striking his hand harshly against his leg. 'How else was I expected to feel when I heard that my wife had run off with another man and that she was pregnant with that man's child?'

'She told you what?' It was starting to make sense.

'It killed me, Tash.'

'I can imagine.' She paused. 'You do know that Lily *is* your child?'

'Yes. I can see it so clearly. It's also clear that in that respect my mother lied to me.' He stood and stared unseeingly at her. 'How could a mother who confessed to love her son do something like that?'

'Because it made you need her again.'

'No.'

'Don't you see, Brenton? She needed you to need her. When you had me, you didn't need her, you needed me.'

'No. This can't be right.'

'What did you do next?' she prompted after a moment.

'I searched for you, I searched for this other guy. Nothing. A friend of mine worked at the hospital my mother took you to and he told me you'd been admitted for possible miscarriage and then discharged. He had no idea where you'd disappeared to.'

'It cemented your mother's lies.'

'Yes. I went overseas to a war zone for a few years because I couldn't be around the places that brought back memories of you.'

She shook her head. He'd been hurt so badly—they both had—and all because of his mother.

He held out his hand to her and she hesitated for a moment. Slowly she walked towards him, and when she was within touching distance he grabbed her and pulled her against him, folding her into his arms.

'Tash, I need you to find me that death certificate. Could you do that tomorrow?'

She rested her head against his chest and for a long moment she was content simply to stand there, in his embrace, listening to his heartbeat.

'We've covered a lot of ground tonight.'

'Mmm.'

'You know we really should—'

'Shh. Don't talk.' She snuggled into his chest a bit more and sighed. Brenton rested his chin on top of her head and they both stood quietly.

She wanted time to stand still so she could continue to absorb him. For years she'd dreamed of being held in his arms and slowly, finally she'd forced herself to move on. Now, though, now she could dream all she wanted and right now that dream was coming true. She could hear the pounding of his heart, hear it accelerate as his breathing became intensified. The attraction was there, the deep physical need to reach the ultimate in fulfilment, and it was something she'd only experienced with Brenton.

As he held her, all rational thought started to slip from his mind. He knew he should tell Tash that he'd contacted his solicitor but all he wanted to do was to hold her—protect her. The feel of her against him and the way she turned his insides to mush was all he could focus on for now.

'Tash?' When she didn't reply he continued. 'Tash, if we continue standing here for much longer, I'm not going to be able to contain myself.'

She pulled back slightly and looked up at him.

'Can't you feel it?' He drew her back to the circle of his arms, moulding her body to his. 'We fit,' he murmured in her ear, causing goose-bumps to spread over her body. 'So perfectly.' His arms came around her waist, his hands sliding up her back to her nape. There his fingers removed the hairpins, instinctively knowing where each one would be placed. They dropped heedlessly to the floor.

He unwound her ponytail before carefully sliding the band away, her auburn locks tumbling down. Natasha closed her eyes, arched her neck and slightly shook her head. His fingers threaded themselves through the soft, silkiness of her hair while he bent his head to press hot butterfly kisses on her long, smooth neck.

'Mmm,' she murmured, before parting her lips.

Brenton just couldn't help himself. He need to feel her skin beneath his lips, to feel her body pressed against his. It felt so right, how could it be so wrong? For years he'd fought feeling anything for her except disdain yet now…now… having her here, melting in his arms, making that little moaning sound in the back of her throat…it was more than he could bear.

He wanted more. He wanted it all. All of Tash, all the time. Moving in with them was the right decision, he admitted, because the feelings she was evoking in him now were only a taste of what he knew could happen, and the thought was starting to drive him insane.

His lips had caressed either side of her neck and now he dipped lower…covering the exposed part of her upper chest with kisses. Natasha's fingers threaded themselves through his hair as she arched back further, allowing him access to her body.

Each kiss felt as though it were an electric charge which set off a series of explosions inside her. He knew just what to do, just how to excite her, and he was obviously going to use that knowledge against her. At least, she hoped he would.

Slowly, he started working his way up. 'Do you think,' he murmured between kisses, 'Jude would notice if we sneaked into your room?'

'Brenton!' She lifted his head away so she could look at him.

His laugh was rich and full, the sound washing over her, heightening her awareness even more. He stood to his full height and gathered her to him for a moment, allowing their breathing to return to a more normal pace.

Eventually, he pulled back and took her hands in his. He knew he was rushing her—himself, *both* of them—and he desperately tried to slow the pace.

'All right.' He tugged her out of the room. 'I'll go home but…' Brenton stopped in the hallway, his eyes looking down into hers '…you have to promise to dream of me.' His gaze was still filled with desire and she could feel herself succumbing. She took a step back, only to find herself pressed against the wall.

He raised a hand to her face and caressed her cheek before his thumb rubbed lightly across her parted lips. Her heart pounded faster and butterflies took flight in her stomach. 'You're beautiful,' he whispered. 'I don't think you have any idea just how beautiful you are.'

Her eyes widened at his words and her heart rate, which had just started to return to its normal rhythm, started to pick up the pace again. He was going to kiss her—a *real* kiss. The first *real* kiss since their last kiss goodbye at the airport over seven years ago.

'Brenton.' Natasha looked up at him as he shifted closer, one hand on the wall beside her, the other still caressing her cheek.

'Why the hesitation, Tash?' The deep rumble of his words ignited the fire once more. 'You want it. I want it.' He rubbed his thumb over her lips again and she closed her eyes in confusion.

'You still don't believe I'm telling the truth,' she choked out, moving her head slightly from side to side. She swallowed the lump in her throat, her breathing increasing even more as the tip of his nose brushed hers.

'Does it matter what I believe? What I *feel* for you...' He breathed out harshly and her eyes snapped open. She met his gaze. The desire had only intensified. 'What I feel for you, Tash...it's burning me up inside. I can't sleep, I can't think straight and every time I see you, regardless of where it is, I just want to rip your clothes off and relive one memory after another.'

She gasped at his words. It was the same for her. The strength, the sheer animalistic urge to follow those feelings to a natural conclusion only grew with each moment she spent with him.

His thumb rubbed across her lips once more before he brought his fingers beneath her chin, tilting her face upwards.

'I need this.' The three words were wrenched deep from within him, their breath mingling in sweet anticipation.

His lips were warm and soft on her own and for a split second he made no further move as though he was savouring every nanosecond. She opened her mouth a little more, inviting him to continue, and with a hungry groan he increased the pressure.

He shifted his feet, bringing their bodies into contact, and the heat from him flooded through her as he brought his other hand up to cup her face. The wanting, the needing…the passion. They were the same mix as they'd been all those years ago and the concoction proved to be as lethal as it always had been.

Lily called out in her sleep and Brenton immediately pulled back, startled by the sound. He looked over his shoulder towards Lily's door, only to have Natasha turn his face back to her.

'Don't worry. She's just talking in her sleep.' Looping one hand behind his head, she urged him closer.

'Tash. Wait.'

'No. You started this, Brenton, now finish it. Properly.'

'But Lily—'

'Always talks in her sleep.' Natasha raised herself up on tiptoe and captured his lips with hers. It took him a moment to realise she meant business. He threaded his arms around her waist and brought her back against his body. When she moaned with delight, he almost capitulated. It would be so easy to pick her up and carry her through to her bed.

'Well, I see you two have everything you need for the night,' Aunt Jude drawled as she walked up the hallway from the kitchen.

They sprang apart like guilty teenagers and Natasha felt her face flushing with embarrassment. She risked a quick glance at Brenton, only to see him grinning.

'Well—almost,' he said with a laugh.

Embarrassment washed over her and as Aunt Jude entered her own room Natasha covered her face with her hands.

Brenton was still chuckling. 'Come on, Tash. It's not
hat bad.'

'That's what you think,' she muttered, but dropped her
hands. Opening the door, she motioned for him to go.

'Kicking me out?'

'Yes.'

His laugh was deep and rich. 'All right. I'll go but remember…' he pressed his lips teasingly to hers '…to dream about
me because I know I'll be dreaming about you, and I sincerely
doubt we'll get as much sleep apart as we would together!'
He kissed her once more before opening the screen door and
leaving.

Natasha leaned against the closed door and sighed. Nothing
had changed. Physically, nothing between them had changed,
but were they strong enough not to get too involved before
sorting everything else out? She doubted it. She doubted it
very much.

CHAPTER NINE

FOR the next two days, Natasha was rostered on to do night which gave her far too much time to think about her past a well as trying to second-guess what her future might or migk not hold. Brenton would definitely be in her life—after all, h was Lily's father and he had just as much right to their daugh ter as she did—but what would her relationship be with him Friend? Casual kissers? Something more?

She smothered a yawn and leaned back in the chair befor taking another sip of her coffee. It was almost half past fou in the morning and at the moment A & E was nice and quie Unfortunately, it gave her time to think about Brenton an their situation.

The attraction was there and it was definitely mutual, bu was the attraction enough? She'd already grieved for hir once. What if something were to happen to him again? Woul she be able to cope? And what about Lily?

Around and around in her head the thoughts went, so muc so that she seemed to have a constant headache. Workin nights meant she was up to supervise Lily in the mornin sleeping all day long so she could spend time with Lily in th afternoon.

Brenton, too, was able to spend time with Lily, which wa good for their father-daughter relationship. He'd eaten dinne with them ever since Wednesday night and the meals wer starting to radiate that 'family' atmosphere Natasha ha craved for most of her life.

Tonight, once Lily had gone to bed, she and Brenton ha sat down to watch a movie on television, simply content t spend some quiet time together. It had been relaxing and en

oyable, reinforcing how strong their friendship had been in
he past.

When the movie had finished, he'd helped Natasha sort
hrough the boxes where she kept her official papers and fi-
ally they'd found the death certificate. Neither of them had
wanted to look at it, knowing it represented the lies that had
ept them apart for so long.

Afterwards, Natasha had started getting ready for work.
Brenton had walked her to the door and taken her hand in
his.

'We need to talk,' he'd murmured. 'Not only about me
moving in but other things, too.'

'I know.'

He'd bent and brushed his lips across hers. The kiss had
been feather-light but had held a strong sense of possessive-
ness which both touched and surprised her. 'Have a good
night. Drive safely.'

It had been the first time he'd kissed her since Jude had
caught them on Friday night and even though the touch had
been brief, it sent her mind reeling. How was she supposed
to concentrate?

'Just had a call,' Deb said as she walked into the tearoom,
bringing Natasha back to the present. 'From the Barwon Gaol
n Lara. One of the prisoners has overdosed and they're bring-
ng him in. I've already called Brenton and asked him to come
n.'

'Why? I'm sure we can handle it.' She wasn't ready to see
him just yet. What if the night remained quiet? He might want
o have that 'talk'!

'Hospital protocol. Because we're the hospital closest to the
gaol, it means we treat any prisoners requiring hospitalisation.
The deal is that the director or head of each unit must sign
off on the paperwork to keep everything above board.'

'Surely Brenton can do that when he comes in for his shift.'

Deb shrugged. 'I'm just following protocol.'

Natasha sighed heavily and drained her cup before stand-
ng. 'Any idea what the prisoner took?'

'Not at this stage. They should be here in about ten mor minutes so I thought I'd better grab a cup of coffee while it' quiet.'

Natasha nodded and started out of the room.

'Uh, Natasha?' Deb said hesitantly. Natasha turned to loo at her, eyebrows raised in question. 'Is it true about you an Brenton?'

'Is *what* true?'

'That you used to be married?' Natasha nodded. 'So doe that mean he's got some sort of…dark side that we neve see?'

'No.' She was puzzled.

'Well, I'm just curious why you divorced him—in fac most of the staff are. He may be aloof and a bit stand-offis at times but seeing him with the patients shows he's a sof touch at heart and, believe me, he's *the* most eligible bachelc at the hospital. I think he's been asked to the hospital fund raiser by almost every single nurse in the hospital.'

'Really? What…what fundraiser? He doesn't usually lik all the fuss and bother.' At least, she thought, he didn't in th past, but now that he was the director of A & E he woul probably be required to attend.

'In a few weeks. It's the hospital's biggest event of th year. Anyway, he's turned every invitation down. We a thought he'd take Annie—you know, because they've know each other for so long—but now that you've appeared on th scene, I'm not so sure.'

'Meaning?'

Deb laughed. 'The tension when the two of you are in th same room is electric and the question on nearly everyone' lips is…why? Why did you divorce him?'

Natasha cleared her throat, feeling more than a little un comfortable. She squared her shoulders and raised her chi 'I didn't divorce him.' Her statement was matter-of-fact, an at the puzzled expression on Deb's face she was momentaril tempted to explain but decided against it. Instead, she swal lowed the lump which had formed in her throat and heade

out the room, trying to focus her thoughts on different scenarios with their incoming patient.

She entered Trauma Room 1 where the patient would be
brought and went through a check-list of drugs and equipment
necessary for reviving a patient from a drug overdose.

The ambulance pulled up outside and she headed in its
direction. Prison guards came through the door first and it was
then she noticed the hospital security guards coming forward
to shake hands with them. Well, at least that angle was taken
care of.

She walked forward to meet the paramedics and to get an
update but one of the prison guards held a hand out to stop
her. 'I'm the doctor,' she said forcefully, and waited for him
to remove his hand. He didn't. 'I need to get to my patient.'

'All in good time, Doctor.'

She glared at him before turning her attention to the paramedics who were pulling the trolley from the ambulance.
'Status.'

'Toby Koop. Twenty-two-year-old male. We've revived
him twice with Narcan,' one of the paramedics said as they
wheeled him inside, the guards standing close by. The patient
had an oxygen mask over his face and an IV line in his arm.
Natasha pushed through, pressing her fingers to the man's
carotid pulse as she went, finding it slow. All of her staff
were gowned and gloved, following the hospital 'extra pre-
cautions' protocol when dealing with drug overdose patients.

'What was he taking?' She reached for a torch and checked
his pupils.

'Not quite sure,' the guard answered, 'but there's been a
few reported cases of heroin in the gaol.'

Natasha nodded, acknowledging the information. 'Pupils
constricted. Pretty high-octane stuff?'

'Yep.'

'Looks as though he injected it through a vein in the top
of his hand,' the paramedic added, and pointed to the site.

'Do we know how much?' The nurses were taking off
Toby's clothes and getting him into a hospital gown.

'The syringe was three mg. Can't say how much was in there, though,' the guard answered.

'Let's get him hooked up to an ECG to watch for dysrhythmias. Continue with oxygen and IV saline.'

'Pulse has gone,' one of the nurses stated urgently.

'Breathing stopped,' another confirmed. Natasha was at Toby's head so she ripped off the oxygen mask, checked his airway was clear, tipped his head back and held out her hand for the manual respirator. She placed the mouth-nosepiece in position before squeezing.

'Crash trolley,' she ordered, indicating for the nurse to take over from her. 'Defib paddles. Charge to two hundred.' While Natasha waited for the paddles to be charged, the nursing staff continued with their CPR until she was ready.

'Is…is he gonna be OK?' the guard asked.

'If you could just wait outside,' one of the nurses said.

'No. I can't.'

'Then be quiet,' Natasha snapped. 'Paddles charged.' The gel pads were on the patient's chest. 'All clear,' she called, and applied the paddles. She held her breath.

'Yep. We've got one. Pulse has returned.'

'Right.' She handed the paddles back to the nurse and helped set up the ECG. 'Ten mg Narcan, stat.' Toby came around moments later, his eyes fluttering open, and he sat up spontaneously but allowed the nursing staff to ease him back

'It's all right, Toby,' Natasha soothed. 'I'm Dr Forest and you're in Geelong General Hospital.' He looked at her, his eyes still glazed, before turning a lovely shade of green

'Bucket,' she called, and stepped out of the way just in time as Toby vomited. Thankfully, the bucket caught most of it, the stench filling the room almost unbearable.

He lay back on the bed and closed his eyes. 'We're monitoring your heartrate, Toby, and you're also having your fluids topped up, which will help bring your blood pressure back to normal.'

'No use explaining to him, Doc,' the guard said. 'He knows what he's done. He's had a few overdoses in his time.'

'Thank you,' she replied in a clipped tone. The nurses did the obs again and reported their findings. His pulse was stronger, his skin wasn't quite so clammy and the ECG reading was almost normal. 'Keep him here for a while and notify CCU he'll be up soon.' Natasha walked over to the sink and stripped off her gloves, gown and mask before heading out of the room. As she came through the curtain, she was accosted by another of the nursing staff.

'Oh, Natasha, I was just coming to get you. A patient has presented with a stab wound to his upper right arm.'

'Via ambulance?'

'No. He apparently drove himself in. I've just put him in TR-2.'

'Thanks.' Natasha nodded and walked into TR-2. Deb and another nurse were with the patient and were removing his shirt to give better access to the wound site. Natasha picked up the notes and read the details taken by the triage sister. Robert Kopel was a thirty-three-year-old divorced male who said he'd tripped in the kitchen and had fallen on a knife, which had lacerated his upper right arm.

'Mr Kopel?'

'Yes.' He was clean-shaven with short blond hair and brown eyes.

'I'm Dr Forest. I understand you've had a bit of an accident tonight?'

'Yes.' He pointed to the folder she was holding. 'I told the nurse all about it.'

Natasha nodded and put the notes down. 'Would you mind telling me as well? Please?' She smiled at him.

'Well…I was um…in the kitchen, getting some food—'

'At four o'clock in the morning?'

'I'm a shift worker. I only got home just before four.'

'I see. Please, continue.'

'I…well, I was chopping up some vegetables and when I put the knife down, it was kind of on the corner of the bench, I guess. Anyway, I turned away to the stove and when I turned back, I tripped over the cat, which sent me stumbling towards the bench. I knocked the knife off the bench and then as I fell, the knife did, too, and I kind of landed on it with it going into my arm.'

She nodded again. 'Where do you work?'

'At the power plant.'

'I see. What type of vegetables were you chopping?'

'Pumpkin—I'd already chopped the potatoes.' He gave a little nervous laugh. 'You know what it's like coming home from shift work, you want a good solid meal, just like any ordinary nine-to-five worker would have in the evening after they'd come home from work.'

'Sure. I understand.' Natasha washed her hands and pulled on a pair of gloves. She walked over and glanced at the dressing Deb had just removed and placed on the trolley. 'Did you put that dressing on by yourself?' She returned her attention to his wound site.

'Yes.'

'You're very resourceful. Have you taken anything for the pain?'

'Uh…just paracetamol tablets, but I *am* in a bit of pain.'

'OK. We'll get you sorted out.' She examined the wound, frowning a little. The wound was deeper than she'd expected, as though the knife had penetrated his arm with a lot more force than Mr Kopel was admitting to. 'Did you fall onto this hand?' she asked him as she took a look at his right wrist.

'Ah, no. No. I kind of just…fell.' She nodded and checked his other wrist. 'Why are you looking there? Up here is where it hurts the most.' He gestured to the wound.

'Of course,' she replied, somewhat surprised by his sudden agitation. 'I need to give you a local anaesthetic, just around the wound site here, and that should help take away some of the pain. Do you know what time you took the paracetamol?'

'Straight after it happened, which is well over an hour ago now. I really think I need something else for the pain. Really I do.'

'OK. We'll give you something a bit stronger.' She took off her gloves and wrote instructions in the notes, as well as authorising some medication for Mr Kopel. She washed her hands and pulled on a gown, mask and fresh gloves before taking another look at his wound. The bleeding had stopped and she glanced down his arms, looking for signs of needle marks. There weren't any. Mr Kopel was on edge about something and his story about his injury wasn't sitting right with her. Arms weren't the only places junkies could inject themselves. She smiled at him. 'Are you sure you didn't hurt your legs—knees, ankles—when you fell?'

He shrugged. 'Yeah. Of course I did but they're all right now—uh, except they are aching quite a bit. I guess you should really give me something for the pain right now.'

'Whereabouts is the pain, exactly?'

'What? Don't you believe me?'

'Of course I do.' He was acting strangely and this wasn't something she was about to discount. 'I'm merely asking so I can make a diagnosis. I'd like to take a look at them so if you could take off your trousers, that would be the first step.'

'I'm not undressing in front of you lot,' he remarked savagely, glaring from one woman to the other.

'Would you like me to call a male nurse?'

'No. No.'

'Mr Kopel, I can't help noticing that you're rather on edge. Are you sure everything is all right?'

He seemed to relax but only just a fraction. 'Yeah, yeah. Course I am. I'm just…you know…in shock. Yeah, shock, that's it, and I think it's terrible that you're not giving me anything for the pain.'

Deb held out a small medicine cup to him which contained two little white pills. In her other hand, she had a glass of water.

'What's this?' Mr Kopel asked.

'Something stronger for the pain,' Natasha confirmed.

'What is it?' He turned his nose up at the tablets in disgust.

'Paracetamol and codeine.'

'What? I'll need something stronger than that.'

'This will help take away the pain you're feeling, and once

we get the local anaesthetic into your arm, that should help as well.' As she spoke, the nurse brought over the tray of instruments she would need. 'The sooner you take the tablets, the sooner the pain will decrease,' she said as he sat there, not moving.

'I'm *not* taking those tablets!' He swiped at Deb with his left arm, knocking the medicine cup upwards out of her hand, and water sprayed over the floor. In the next instant he'd reached into his trouser pocket and had pulled out a small gun. He aimed it at Natasha.

Deb screamed.

Mr Kopel slipped off the bed and stood behind Natasha, the cold edge of the gun pressing against her neck.

'Give me something stronger. *Now!*' he yelled.

Natasha froze. For a whole second, which seemed to last an eternity, she was completely frozen to the spot. This man— this clean-shaven, seemingly respectable man—had pulled a gun on her and was demanding stronger pain relief! Unbelievable!

She took a deep, calming breath, knowing she had to keep her head. It was very hard when all she could hear was the pounding of her heartbeat reverberating in her ears. Her mouth went dry and she quickly swallowed. 'What did you have in mind?' Was that *her* voice sounding so calm and professional?

'Morphine or…or pethidine or something strong like that. Come on, I know you can authorise it so do it.'

'Get him ten mg of morphine,' she told the nurse.

'Just don't try to be a hero,' he warned as the nurses edged towards the curtain. 'And get those curtains open,' he ordered. 'Wide open so I can see everyone. And you'd better be back quickly or your doctor friend here gets it.'

As the curtains were opened, one of the prison guards could be seen heading their way. 'I heard a scream,' he said to the nurse who had just pushed the curtain back. He then turned and looked at Natasha.

'A cop!' Mr Kopel whispered so only Natasha could hear

She also heard the thread of fear in his voice. The prison guard immediately went for his gun but it was too late. Mr Kopel moved the gun away from Natasha for a split second, long enough to point it at the guard and fire.

The sound was deafening and the guard immediately doubled over, grasping his abdomen. A scream rose in Natasha's throat at the unexpected turn of events and escaped from her mouth. The other staff in the area all dropped to the floor in fright.

Natasha was too shaken to realise the gun was now back, pointing at her throat, and she could feel the heat emanating from it. One of the nurses was still screaming.

'Shut up! Shut up!' Mr Kopel yelled. 'Someone get me some drugs—*now!*'

'What on earth is going on here?' a male voice said from one side. Natasha moved her eyes, not her head, and saw Brenton. Toby Koop was sleeping off his own drug side-effects and a nurse crouched on the floor beside his bed. The other prison guard was on the floor also, ready to shoot.

Natasha continued to look around at the sight before her, her gaze finally resting on Brenton who was heading slowly towards the injured guard.

'Stay away from him,' Mr Kopel warned.

'Don't be ridiculous,' Brenton muttered. 'This man needs medical attention.'

'He's right.' Natasha forced herself to speak. Brenton was putting himself right in the line of fire and that was the last thing she wanted. There was no way she was going to let him get shot, not if she could help it. 'Mr Kopel—Robert,' she soothed. 'That man is not a police officer. He's a prison guard. See? See that man over there on the bed? He's a prisoner.'

'Stay away from him,' Mr Kopel said again.

'Dr Worthington is right. The guard needs attention or he'll die, Robert. Look at the amount of blood that's on the floor around him. He's losing it too fast. We need to stabilise him.'

'I just—want—my *drugs!*' He stared at the nurse who'd

been on her way to initially get him his fix. 'You. Get going.' The nurse scuttled off.

Natasha watched as Brenton edged closer to the guard.

'I said leave him. You can fix him up once I get my shot.'

'It might be too late.'

'Come on, Robert. Think what will happen if he dies,' Natasha said softly, and felt the end of the barrel of the gun press harder into her neck. She kept quiet, her gaze fixed intently on Brenton. Her heart rate had started to decrease but now it was rising again as she watched Brenton continue to edge towards the guard.

He looked at her, his expression a complete mask, but she knew he could see the fear in her eyes. She wanted to tell him that it wasn't for herself but for him. For him! She loved him. The revelation didn't surprise her but rather comforted her. She'd always loved him and knew that she desperately needed him back in her life—as her husband.

Yet now, if they couldn't calm Mr Kopel down, goodness knew *what* would happen. If Brenton got hurt... Tears started to well in her eyes and she blinked them away. She'd already grieved for him once and she wasn't going to do it again.

Not like this.

Not when they'd found each other again.

'Come on, Mr Kopel,' Brenton said as he crouched down close to the guard.

'All right. Get him onto a bed and fix him up, but don't try any funny stuff or the lady doc gets it.'

'How's your arm, Robert?' she asked quietly, as Brenton and a few of the nurses slid the guard onto a pat-slide and managed to transfer him to the bed. Brenton was snapping out orders left, right and centre, asking for surgeons and anaesthetists to be paged. The department became a hive of activity and, given their present circumstances, it was an incredible sight.

'It'll be fine once I get my drugs.'

'Did you really fall on the knife, Robert?'

'You're a smart lady. I'm sure you've already figured out that I didn't.'

'You stabbed yourself intentionally so you could come in here for a fix.'

'Only *you*...' he pressed the gun against her neck once more '...wouldn't give it to me.'

'Well, it should be here soon.'

'What's taking so long?' he asked between gritted teeth.

'There's a hospital protocol which needs to be followed every time drugs are authorised. Morphine isn't usually kept in A & E,' she lied, 'so the nurse will have to get it from the pharmacy downstairs. It needs to be signed and triple-checked by two nurses and all of that takes time but, rest assured, it is coming.'

'You'd better hope so. It's your insurance policy.'

A man walked into the room wearing a white coat and Mr Kopel shifted uneasily. 'Who's that?' he asked, alarmed, and then said more forcefully, 'Who are you?'

'I'm Dr Jamieson,' the man said without looking up. 'The surgeon.' He washed his hands and pulled on a pair of gloves, then joined Brenton and his team. Although Natasha was new here, she frowned a little at the man's reply. This man *wasn't* Paul Jamieson.

Natasha turned her gaze back to Brenton and saw him glance in her direction. She saw the anguish and hesitation in his eyes and knew a plan was definitely in progress—but what?

'I want my *drugs!*' Mr Kopel yelled. He took the gun away from Natasha's neck momentarily and pointed it towards where Brenton was standing. Natasha froze—not wanting to watch but unable to look away. 'What are you giving that guy? Don't give it to him, give it to me. *Now!*'

A loud explosion came from behind her and she watched as Brenton crumpled to the floor.

No! she tried to say, but found she couldn't. He'd shot Brenton!

A split second later there seemed to be more gunfire and

Natasha wrenched herself free from Mr Kopel's hold. She tried to move fast, tried to shift out of the way. A scream lodged itself in her throat and stayed there as she suddenly felt blinding pain in her left arm.

Her knees folded beneath her and she dropped to the floor, her mind registering one fact and one alone.

Brenton had been shot!

Brenton was dead!

CHAPTER TEN

IT HAD happened again! Brenton had died—*again!*

Natasha closed her eyes in pain, unable to block the sight of him from her mind. Even though she'd been calm, even though she'd tried her best to control the situation so he didn't get hurt, nothing had gone right.

Brenton was dead.

The words were reverberating around in her head, making her feel dizzy and nauseated. She tried to open her eyes again but found she couldn't. People were moving around her but she couldn't understand what they were saying.

Besides…what did it matter? Brenton was dead.

'Tash? Tash?'

'She's unconscious, Brenton, but her pulse is stable,' Deb reported, as he watched several members of staff rally around Natasha.

Brenton allowed himself to be helped to his feet. The police were everywhere, checking out Mr Kopel, their guns trained on him in case he moved, but Brenton knew the man was dead. He stared at his lifeless form. The police officer who'd posed as Dr Jamieson had returned fire, along with the prison guard, after Natasha had crumpled to the floor.

Never in his life had he felt so helpless as he had at that moment. When he'd walked into the treatment area to see her being held hostage he'd been so consumed with rage he'd been hard pressed to control the urge to walk over and deal with Mr Kopel himself. Thankfully logic had prevailed but it still hadn't prevented the woman he loved being shot.

His mouth was dry and he swallowed, his gaze fixed on

Natasha. Someone was fussing over him, checking where the bullet had grazed the side of his temple. He pulled away.

'We need to check you over, Brenton.'

'I'm fine. Have the triage sister deal with the police and Mr Kopel. Let me know if there are any problems.' Without waiting for a response, Brenton walked over to where Natasha was lying on a bed. He moved in and was glad when no one stopped him. Tenderly he brushed his fingers across her cheek and then let his thumb trail over her lips. 'How bad is her arm?'

'It looks as though the bullet passed straight through the humerus,' the other registrar on duty was saying.

Brenton nodded. 'Obs?'

'BP is stable, we're putting in an IV to replace blood loss,' Deb reported. 'Pulse has improved and, to tell you the truth, Brenton, she has all the signs of fainting. We'll monitor her for shock.'

'Of course.' He watched as Natasha's arm was bandaged and felt the carotid pulse at her neck. 'She saw me get shot.' He nodded again. It made sense. She'd fainted the last time she'd thought he'd died. Why shouldn't this time, in these heightened circumstances, when she'd thought he'd been shot, be any different? 'How soon will the real Dr Jamieson be here?'

'About another five minutes.'

'Good. Get the prisoner up to CCU, call the director of orthopaedics for Natasha and get her organised for Radiology. How's the prison guard?' He looked over his shoulder into TR-3, where the prison guard was being well looked after.

'BP is climbing to a more steady level, pupils are fine, pulse is thready but we're monitoring it closely and oxygen saturation is improving.'

'Get him in for radiographs so we can see exactly where that bullet is.' Brenton nodded to the registrar. 'You take the guard. I'll stay with Tash.'

'Brenton, I don't think—'

'There's no argument,' Brenton snapped, but the registrar stood his ground. 'I'm not going to operate on her, Doctor, I'm just going to monitor her. She's my wife!'

The registrar hesitated for a moment before nodding, leaving Brenton with Natasha.

'It's quite legal for you to treat her, Brenton,' Deb said softly as she sponged Natasha's forehead. 'After all, you are divorced.'

'No.' He shook his head but didn't say more. He looked down at the woman of his dreams. His heart knew the truth. Natasha *was* his wife—legally. He bent over and brushed his lips across Natasha's. 'Tash? Honey?' He patted her cheek lightly and lovingly. 'Come on, Tash.' He kissed her again, feeling tears prick behind his eyes. 'It's all right. I'm OK. Tash? I'm OK and so are you.'

Natasha stirred. She could hear Brenton's voice talking softly to her, telling her everything was OK. She squeezed her eyes tight shut. She didn't want to open them. She didn't want to wake from this dream into the reality she knew would be…meaningless. Emotions, one after the other, started to swamp her. She'd felt them all before and during the last seven and a half years she'd been positive she'd worked through them all. She didn't want them again. Feelings of loss, helplessness and utter desolation.

'Tash? Come on, Tash. Open your eyes. It's all right.'

She felt a kiss brush across her lips—Brenton's kiss. She breathed in, her senses registering his unique scent. Oh, this dream was too real, too vivid. She'd had them before, though, and knew the pain opening her eyes would present.

But she had to.

She knew it was the right thing to do. After all, Lily needed her.

With great effort, she forced her lids to open, her gaze

fuzzy and a little out of focus. She frowned and blinked a few times.

'B.J.?'

'Aw, honey.' His hands cupped her face before he pressed his lips firmly to hers. She tried to move her arms, to hold him, but found herself restricted and moaned in pain.

He broke free. 'What's wrong? Did I hurt you?' His gaze was eagerly searching her face.

'My arms?'

'Just keep them still. You're hooked up to an IV and the other arm is bandaged. Get some morphine requested for her,' he told Deb, before returning his attention to Natasha. He gazed down at her, wishing he could wipe the tension from her face. She'd already suffered enough in the past and now she had new emotional scars to add to her collection. If only he could have spared her from them, he would have. He paused and took a breath. 'Do you remember anything?'

She thought for a second and then gasped. 'You were shot.'

'No.' He shook his head, glad her mental clarity was still intact.

He smiled down at her and it was then she saw the gash of dried red blood on the side of his face. 'Yes!' Her eyes opened wide in surprise and her heart rate increased. She tried to sit up but he gently urged her back down.

'It's just a small graze.' He shook his head. 'I'm all right.'

Relief welled up from deep within her. She could feel it bubbling up and over, almost to the point of hysteria. 'You're…you're all right? Really all right? You're not dead.' The words broke on a sob and she shuddered.

'No, honey. I'm not. Shh. It's OK. I'm very much alive and so are you.' He bent and pressed a kiss to her lips again. 'Everything's going to be great, Tash.'

'Sorry to interrupt this most touching scene,' Deb said from beside them, and it was the first Natasha realised they had an audience. She laid her head back on the bed and closed her eyes as a wave of embarrassment flooded over her. 'But I have some pain relief here for you and then it's time for X-rays.'

Natasha's eyes snapped open and she looked at Brenton. He slipped his hand into hers and gave it a little squeeze. 'I'm not going to leave you,' he promised, interpreting the look in her eyes.

She relaxed a little, glad he was staying.

Deb administered the pain relief and then flicked off the brakes on the hospital bed. 'All righty, then,' the nurse said in a sing-song voice. 'Off to Radiology we go.'

'How's the prison guard?' Natasha asked as she was wheeled along.

'Stabilised and waiting for the real Dr Jamieson,' Brenton replied.

'And the prisoner? Toby? Is he still OK?'

'On his way to CCU.'

This seemed to relax Natasha—the general chit-chat—rather than focusing on what had happened with Mr Kopel. 'I've called in two more registrars to help cover the work-load,' Brenton ventured, still holding her right hand as they walked along. 'More nursing staff have been requested, as well as counsellors. Oh, and your ortho consultant should be here once we get back from Radiology.'

'Good.' She closed her eyes as the bright artificial lights continued to appear and disappear overhead as she was wheeled along. Brenton came into Radiology with her and again helped her to get into position for the X-ray of her arm.

'I want you to see a counsellor, too,' he said.

'I'd presumed it would be hospital protocol.' She sighed.

'It is.'

'I'm sick of counsellors.'

'I can understand that.'

'I don't know if you can. I was seeing a counsellor for

years. I don't think I've ever got over you.' The words were said softly and she held his gaze.

'I know how you feel.' He bent and pressed his lips to hers. 'Tonight has helped put a lot of things into perspective.'

'Here are your X-rays. All done,' the radiologist said as he held them out to Brenton. 'You've been very lucky, Natasha.'

Brenton held the X-rays up to the light so Natasha could see. The bullet had made a hole in her arm, shattering bits of her humerus, but nothing too bad. 'I think the orthopaedic blokes will have you back to normal in no time at all,' he prophesied. 'Let's get you back to A & E and get an Emergency Theatre booked.'

She closed her eyes as she was once more wheeled back to A & E. 'How long do you think I'll be in Theatre?'

'I'm not sure. We'll have to check with Brian.'

'Who's he again?'

'He's the director of orthopaedics. Brian Newton. You may not have met him yet. Nice guy.'

'So you trust him?' Natasha could feel herself getting more tired by the second.

'Absolutely.'

'Brenton?' The barouche stopped moving and she tried to open her eyes but found her lids were as heavy as a ton of bricks.

'What is it, honey?'

'Getting shot makes you very sleepy.'

He chuckled. 'I'm sure it does. Rest now.' He pressed his lips to hers, inwardly rejoicing at being able to touch her. 'I'll give Jude a call and let her know what's happened.'

'No,' she protested weakly. 'Don't worry her.'

'I have to tell her, Tash. You're going to be in hospital for at least the next few days, depending on how quickly you recover.'

Natasha moved her head slightly on the pillow. 'I don't want Lily to see me like this.'

'Don't worry. Jude and I will take care of everything.' He bent his head and whispered close to her ear, 'You just concentrate on getting better because we need you, Tash. *I* need you.'

Upon hearing that, Natasha gave in to the wave of sleep which had been tugging at her. Still, even as she started to dream, a hint of concern remained. Jude and Brenton would take care of everything. They'd take care of Lily—and they'd be doing it *without* her.

She didn't want to be left out. She wanted—no, *needed*— to be a part of everything that concerned Lily. It had been that way since the moment she'd found out she'd been pregnant. How would Lily cope when she heard about the shooting? Natasha didn't want her to worry. She wanted to grab her daughter and wrap her up in cotton wool—right next to herself.

Yet Jude and Brenton were going to take care of everything. They were going to break the awful news to Lily. They'd look after her day and night while Natasha was stuck in the hospital. Lily would be experiencing new things, growing and changing, and Natasha wouldn't be there to see it. A lot could happen in a few days. Just look at the past week!

The thoughts jumbled themselves in her mind and she couldn't seem to shake them. She felt as though she were in a bouncing castle, jumping from one side to the next in very slow motion, trying to get to the end, only to find it took a lifetime to get there. When she finally arrived it was to discover a wall where a door had previously been.

'Tash? Honey?' Brenton's voice was calling to her and she turned in his direction. At last someone had remembered her. At last someone was coming to bring her back into the normal world.

'Tash? Brian's here.'

Natasha opened her eyes, squinting to bring her gaze into

focus. She smiled when she saw Brenton and he caressed her cheek. 'Brian's here,' he told her again.

Brian Newton introduced himself and explained the operation to her. She nodded in all the right places, made impressive murmuring noises and signed the consent form. Then she thankfully laid back on the pillow and closed her eyes again.

She smiled a little as she realised the unique position she was in. She'd explained things, hospital procedures and the like, to patients probably thousands of times, and now she knew how they really felt. They didn't care. All the patients wanted was to get their operations over and done with so they could start getting their lives back on track.

When the anaesthetist came, the same thing happened. She murmured and nodded and gave him the statistical information he needed so he could calculate the correct amount of anaesthetic to administer. Yet all she wanted was to have the operation over and done with, to feel more like herself rather than a numb sack of potatoes, so she could see and hold her daughter. To know for *herself* that Lily accepted what had happened here.

She also knew that Brenton's presence beside her afforded her a great deal of comfort. She knew she didn't need to be too alert when the surgeon and anaesthetist had been talking to her because if anything had been out of line, he would have been on it in a flash.

She loved him so much and he…well, he'd said he *needed* her. Surely that was a good sign. Did it matter that he hadn't said he loved her? He'd said everything would be all right so she'd take that on face value and believe him.

She felt herself being changed out of her work clothes and later remembered asking after the guard and the prisoner once more, but had no idea what the answers had been. Soon she was being wheeled to Theatre, and at the door Brenton kissed her once more.

Had he murmured something in her ear? Had he said he

loved her? She honestly couldn't remember and, anyway, she had an operation to go to. Once the operation was over, she could get on with her life, a life Brenton had promised to be in…hadn't he?

'Will you *please,* stop pacing up and down, Monty? You'll wear a hole in the carpet and then you'll have to find some money in your budget to replace it. Besides, you're giving me neck pain. You're almost as bad as a tennis match.' Annie grinned at him but he kept on pacing.

'How much longer?'

'For the hundredth time—I don't know.'

He stalked around his desk and picked up the phone. Annie was out of her chair like a shot and shoved the receiver back into its cradle. 'Don't.' She stared him down. 'Brian is a re-markably calm and considerate man but if you call through to his Theatre once more and ask what's happening he's going to throttle you and, quite frankly, I don't blame him.' She shook her head and threw her hands up in the air. 'Geez. How did I get lumbered with the babysitting job?'

Brenton raked his hand through his hair yet again, causing his usually straight brown hair to stand on end. 'Just lucky, I guess. When are they going to call?'

'How did Jude take the news?'

'Not well. She was crying on the phone.'

'She's packing a bag of clothes for Tash and bringing it in after she's taken Lily to school.'

'What about Lily?'

'Jude and I decided it's best if we tell her after school today. Together.' His hand worked its way through his hair again. 'I feel so helpless, Annie, and not only with Tash. How am I supposed to tell Lily that her mother has been shot? I have no idea how this child is going to react and I don't think Jude does either.'

'She seems to be a pretty switched-on kid—remember who her mother is.'

He laughed humourlessly. 'True.'

'And look at the way Lily has readily accepted you into her life.'

'That was different. She had Tash as her constant. In the past month that child has left the only home she can remember and moved to Geelong with her mother. Sure, she knew Aunt Jude but she'd only seen her now and then—it was the main reason Tash decided to move in the first place. She's started at a new school, discovered her father is alive and now she has to be told that her mother's been shot!' He shook his head.

'I think you should tell her here.'

'Hmm?'

'Tell Lily here. At the hospital. The first thing she's going to want to do is to see Natasha. So if you tell her *here* then she's not going to have the time to stress and worry. She'll be able to go straight on up to CCU and see her mother.'

Brenton nodded. 'Actually, that's not a bad idea.'

'Thank you. Thank you. Just make sure that Natasha knows about it. She'll be pretty groggy from the anaesthetic still but if her hair is brushed and she has a bit of make-up on her face so she doesn't look so pale, that should help.'

'She'll want to see Lily, I'm sure of it. She was mumbling things before she went into Theatre and I could tell she was concerned about our little girl.' He nodded reassuringly to himself.

'Listen to you.' Annie giggled. '*Our* little girl. That's cute.'

'It's amazing, Annie. That child has wound me around her little finger as well as winding herself around my heart. I can't believe how much I love her.'

'And what about her mother?' Annie asked, all humour gone.

'I've never stopped loving Tash. That was made abundantly clear to me as I watched her fall after she was shot.' He closed his eyes, trying to squeeze the memory away. He shook his head.

'I'm glad you're getting counselling too, Brenton.'

'I'll be fine.'

'It's hospital protocol. You were there. You were involved. Trust me, watching your ex-wife get shot wouldn't be something you could just file away in the memory banks and not give another thought to.'

'She's not my ex-wife.'

'What?' Annie frowned, clearly confused.

'The divorce papers were never filed. Natasha and I are still married.'

'What?' She stared at him, completely dumbfounded.

'We're still married.' He paused, still unable to believe his good fortune. 'I'm in love with the woman I'm married to.'

'Quite unheard of, you realise. To be in love with one's wife is not the normal thing,' Annie jested, but then gasped. 'But what about her other marriage…to that other guy?'

'Hmm.' He frowned. 'My solicitor is looking into it.'

The phone rang and he twisted around to snatch it up. 'Yes?' He nodded to Annie. 'I'll be right there. She's out,' he said, after he'd replaced the receiver.

The corridor seemed longer than usual as he and Annie walked from his office towards Emergency Theatre Recovery. Annie picked up the notes and offered them to him but he shook his head and walked towards Natasha's bed. His eyes never left her for a second, her hair tucked beneath a theatre cap, the IV in her right arm, her left bandaged up.

Never had she looked more beautiful in her life. His wife.

Slowly he reached out and took off her cap, spreading her lovely auburn tresses on the pristine white pillow. Tenderly he brushed a few loose strands from her face, loving the feel of her. His heart swelled with love and pride for this woman. She'd been knocked down so much in the past and he knew, without a doubt, that they'd get through everything else but they'd do it *together*. There was no way he was letting this woman go ever again. She belonged to him and so did their daughter.

He lowered his head and pressed a kiss to her lips.

'I love you, Tash,' he whispered in her ear. He'd said it just before she'd left him for Theatre and now when she returned, and he'd say it again and again—for ever.

'I've arranged for Jude to bring Lily to the hospital in about an hour.'

'Keep her routine as normal as possible,' Natasha said.

'Well, tonight Jude will help her with her homework, give her a bath and get her ready for bed so that when she comes in she can stay a while.'

Natasha nodded. Her mind was still quite sluggish from the anaesthetic, even though she'd come out of theatre ten hours ago. 'I don't want her to worry, Brenton. I don't want her to be upset.'

'I know. Jude brought a bag of things in for you.'

'Jude was here?'

'Yes.' Brenton smoothed her hair away from her face. 'You were sleeping but just seeing you were all right was enough for her.'

'I feel so bad for causing everyone so much worry.'

'Don't,' he implored. 'Don't apologise, Tash. None of this was your fault.' He shook his head and sat down on the edge of the bed, brushing his fingers down her cheek. They stared at each other for a long moment before he smiled slowly. 'You're a very beautiful woman, Natasha.' He leaned in and pressed his lips softly to hers.

Natasha closed her eyes, breathing in the familiar scent of him and enjoying the softness of his mouth. She sighed and her body relaxed. When Brenton pulled back, she didn't open her eyes.

'Have another little rest, honey. We'll give your hair a

brush and put a bit of make-up on you before Lily gets here so you look more like her mummy.'

'OK,' Tash mumbled.

Brenton watched as she drifted off again. It had been this way for most of the day. He'd dealt with his paperwork while she'd slept off the anaesthetic, the CCU nurses under strict instructions to tell him when she'd stirred. He'd lost count of the number of times he'd hurried up the stairwell between CCU and A & E, but he didn't care. At least he'd been close.

He'd also managed to delegate and lighten his workload for the next few weeks so he could spend time not only with Natasha but with Lily as well. It wasn't going to be an easy time but he was determined to get his family through this. When he was sure Natasha was asleep, he headed back to his office.

He knew the hospital was buzzing with the news of what had happened this morning, as well as the fact that Brenton had been kissing Natasha ever since! He didn't care. The hospital could think what it wanted, he knew what he felt and that was all that mattered.

The instant he sat back down behind his desk, the phone rang. 'Dr Worthington,' he said.

'Brenton, it's Jude. Lily and I will be leaving in about fifteen minutes to come in. She's already asked why Natasha wasn't home but I told her we'd be going to the hospital to see her. She's actually quite excited.'

'About coming to the hospital?'

'Yes.'

'So you haven't told her anything?'

'No. Just that Natasha is at the hospital.'

'Good.'

'I don't know how this is going to go, Brenton. I'm very worried about how Lily will take the news.'

'You and me both, but nevertheless I don't want to keep it from her any longer. Tash knows she's coming in so I'll head on back to the ward soon and make sure she's awake and looking her most "mummiest".'

'OK. I'll bring Lily to your office as we planned but…'

When Jude hesitated, Brenton felt apprehension wash over him. 'What is it?'

'She's just so excited about coming to the hospital. She's excited to see where you and Natasha work. With that excitement build-up, I'm afraid the news will come as an even bigger shock.'

Brenton exhaled sharply and raked a hand through his hair. 'There's not a lot we can do, Jude. Bring her in and we'll just have to do the best we can. No doubt Natasha would be the expert on how best to handle this situation.' His pager started beeping.

'Why don't you ask her?' Jude suggested.

'She's got too much to worry about at the moment. I've got to go. See you soon.' He hung up the phone and headed out to the treatment area. He needed to prove to himself that he was capable of handling this parenting crisis. He didn't dispute the fact that Natasha knew Lily better than anyone, but he had to start somewhere. 'You paged me?' he asked the triage sister.

'Yes. One-year-old girl, Teneal Harvard, in EC-4. She was found beneath the sink with the lid off a bottle of bath cleaner.'

Brenton gritted his teeth as an immediate impatience surged through him for the unknown parents. Still, these things happened, even with childproof locks. He flicked through the notes which had already been taken before heading to Examination Cubicle 4.

'Good evening,' he said to the distressed father sitting on the examination bed, cradling his daughter in his arms. 'I'm Dr Worthington.' He smiled at the baby. 'Hello, sweetheart. I understand you've been getting into a bit of mischief?'

'I don't know how it happened,' the father said. 'We've

got two older children so we presume one of them left the door open and then we were busy getting the others organised for bed and homework and everything and then we heard Teneal coughing and found her with bathroom cleaner all over her face.'

Brenton hooked his stethoscope into his ears. 'If you could just lie her down on the bed, I'll take a look at her.' Thankfully, with the weather being hot, Teneal was wearing a thin cotton dress, so Brenton lifted it up so he could listen to her chest.

'Did you bring the cleaner with you?' he asked a moment later.

'No.'

'And you haven't given Teneal anything?'

'No.'

'Was it a creme cleanser or a bleach liquid?'

'Uh…uh…one in a blue bottle.'

'Well, from the look of her mouth, I think we can assume it wasn't a creme cleanser because there's no chalky residue around it. I think it would be advisable to keep the number of the Poisons Information Centre by your phone for quick future reference.'

'Good thinking. Good thinking. We just didn't know what to do so we bundled her into the car and drove her here.'

'I gather from the notes she's not allergic to anything?'

'Not that we know of.'

'Has she vomited?'

'No, she's just been coughing.'

'I don't blame her. Immunisations all up to date?'

'Yes—oh, and she had an ear infection about a month ago.'

'Right.' Brenton had listened to Teneal's chest while the nurse had checked the child's blood pressure, temperature and respiratory rate. All were slightly above normal. 'All right, sweetheart, you're being such a good girl. I need to have a little look in your mouth.' He showed Teneal his penlight

torch and then the tongue depressor. She coughed a little and
Brenton exchanged a glance with the nurse. It was a 'get
ready in case she vomits' look but thankfully Teneal settled
back down again.

He looked inside her mouth. 'Mild perioral and pharyngeal
erythema. Page the paediatric registrar and give her a drink
of milk. As she hasn't vomited, I'm assuming she didn't swal-
low too much of the liquid. Probably thought it tasted horrible, didn't you, sweetheart?' Brenton stroked Teneal's forehead before turning to the baby's father.

'She's been a very lucky girl. She has a case of mild erythema, which means there are little red bumps around her
mouth and throat due to the poison. I think it's best if Teneal
is kept in overnight for observation but the paediatric registrar
will make that call. Once she's had a drink of milk we'll give
her some vinegar and that should help settle things down, or
bring them up. Either way, the situation should be OK.'

Brenton's pager sounded and he quickly checked the number—it was CCU. He reached for Teneal's chart and wrote
up his findings before leaving her in the nursing staff's capable hands.

Two at a time, he took the stairs to CCU, his heart racing
as it had done every time that day just in case something had
gone wrong with Natasha. When he rounded the corner and
entered the large open ward, it was to find her sitting up in
bed, looking much better.

'Hey, good-looking.' His grin was wide as he strolled over.
'That little catnap seems to have done wonders.'

Natasha smiled and he bent to kiss her. 'What's the time?'
she asked, and smothered a yawn.

'Almost six.'

'Lily?'

'She's due here soon so let's get you ready.' He took the
bag which Jude had brought in earlier from her locker and
rummaged through it.

'Do you mind?'

He glanced up and chuckled. 'You must be feeling better if you're indignant with me. I'm only looking for a—ah, here it is.' He pulled out her hairbrush. When Natasha reached out her hand, he shook his head. 'Allow me.'

'Brenton. I don't think now—'

'Now is the perfect time.'

'But what about the staff?'

'What about them?'

'They'll see you brushing my hair!'

'So? They've spent most of the day watching me kiss you and now you're worried about me brushing your hair? Tash, Tash, Tash.' He shook his head and chuckled. 'Let me get you comfortable so I can sit behind you.'

He did just that and started to pull the brush through her beautiful hair. Natasha closed her eyes, giving in to the glorious feeling.

'Brings back memories,' he remarked, his voice husky. Natasha angled her head to look up at him and he kissed the tip of her nose. 'But now is most definitely not the time. There, all done. Painless, wasn't it?'

'For who?' she asked, her eyes filled with repressed memories. Brenton smiled.

'How about some make-up?'

'You're *not* doing that.'

'I agree. You should be able to manage that by yourself.' He dug her make-up bag out and unzipped it. 'I've just seen a one-year-old girl who swallowed some bathroom cleaner,' Brenton remarked as she applied some lipstick.

'Is she all right?'

'Yes. She was lucky but it's driven home to me just how much of Lily's life I've missed.' He looked away, checking his watch as he tried to control his emotions. Natasha reached out and touched his hand.

'You're here now, Brenton. *That's* what's important.'

'I know.' They stared at each other, both understanding the emotions and words which weren't being spoken but were well and truly felt. 'I'm going to stay at your place tonight and move my stuff in tomorrow,' he stated firmly. 'We're a family and we belong together, Tash.'

She nodded and smiled. 'You're right.'

He returned the smile. 'I'd better go and see if they've arrived.' He kissed her before walking from the ward back down to his office.

Jude and Lily were walking through the front door of A & E as he rounded the corner.

'Daddy!' Lily squealed, and rushed towards him. She jumped into his arms and hugged him close. He could feel the odd glance here and there, and when he looked over at the triage sister it was to find her jaw hanging open. He took no notice and gave Lily a kiss.

'Well, hello, there, my princess. How was your day?'

'Uh, OK. Where's Mum?'

Brenton's gaze met Jude's worried one. 'We'll see her in a minute. First, why don't you come and see my office?'

'You've got an office? Cool.' She touched the sticking plaster at his temple. 'What did you do?'

'Why don't we have a look at my office first?' Brenton carried her inside and she scrambled from his arms to go and sit in his chair behind his desk. Both he and Jude sat down watching her. She lifted his phone and opened his drawer and pulled out a piece of paper.

'Can I draw on this?'

'Why don't you come here, first, honey? There's something Aunt Jude and I want to tell you.'

'I want to draw a picture.'

'Later, Lil,' Aunt Jude said in a no-nonsense tone. 'Come here, please.'

Lily reluctantly put down the pen and walked over. Brenton put his arm out for her and she climbed onto his knee.

'Lily…' Why was his mouth suddenly dry? He'd broken bad news to family members time and time again and not once had he felt this nervous. This time, though, it wasn't just any family—it was *his* family. *His* wife. *His* daughter.

'Where's Mum?' she asked again while Brenton was searching for the words. He'd been going over them all day in his head but now…there wasn't an easy way to say what had to be said.

'Lily, there was an accident this morning.'

'Yeah, but you and Mum are doctors and make people better.'

'That's right.' He pointed to his sticking plaster. 'See this? Well, Daddy got a little bit hurt in the accident.' Her eyes widened in alarm and her fingers automatically reached out to touch the sticking plaster.

'Did it hurt?'

He smiled a little and hugged her close, his love for her growing with each passing second. 'It hurt a little bit.' He kissed her cheek and Aunt Jude took hold of her hand. 'But Mummy, well, Mummy got hurt, too.'

Lily looked to Aunt Jude as though begging her to say it wasn't true. 'Where did she get hurt?'

'In her arm.'

'Mum has a sore arm?'

'That's right.'

Lily climbed off his knee and Brenton reluctantly let her go. 'You let my mummy get hurt?' Tears welled in the blue eyes and he felt his heart lurch with pain.

'Lily, I—'

'But you promised me, Dad. You promised me that you would look after me and Mummy. You promised,' she sniffed.

'I know, and I am looking—'

'No, you're not,' Lily shouted, tears streaming down her face. 'I want my mummy.'

Brenton reached out to her but she backed away and ran for the door. She was out so fast he hardly had time to stand up. He raced after her. 'Lily?' he called, but there was no sign of her.

CHAPTER ELEVEN

BRENTON raked his hand impatiently through his hair as he headed up the corridor, his gut wrenching with anguish and fear. Where was she?

'Brenton,' Jude called, and he stopped. She came rushing up. 'Let me look for her. She's hurt and upset.'

'And I would just drive her away again,' he acknowledged glumly. 'Great!' He turned around, his eyes searching. Mentally, he was beating himself up. He knew the hurt look in Lily's eyes would haunt him for a long time and he never, ever wanted to see it there again. He was her father. He was supposed to protect her from getting hurt. He shook his head. He should have discussed this with Natasha but, like a damn fool, he'd had to prove something to his macho ego.

One of the nurses came up. 'Is something wrong, Brenton?'

'I can't find my daughter.'

'Your...*daughter*,' the nurse repeated disbelievingly, her eyebrows raised.

'Yes. She's six, has auburn hair like Tash and blue eyes. She came running out of my office about two seconds ago and appears to have disappeared into thin air.'

'Righto. I'll tell the staff.' The nurse hurried off.

Brenton turned to Jude. 'Keep looking out here in the waiting room. I'll check the examination area just in case she managed to get in there.' He didn't wait for an answer and hurried off, his gaze darting back and forth. Everywhere. He looked everywhere, but there was still no sign of her.

When he returned to the waiting room, it was to find Jude sitting there with Lily on her lap. The little girl's head was buried in Jude's shoulder and she was sobbing. Relief washed over him but the sound of his daughter crying was enough to destroy him completely. When Jude saw him, she held up a hand for him to stop where he was. He did. She shook her head and the pain increased.

Jude pointed up, indicating she was going to take Lily up to CCU. Brenton nodded once before turning and striding back to his office. He paced the floor, raking a hand through his hair in agitation.

Lily had been right. *Why* hadn't he protected Natasha better? He'd done his best but it obviously hadn't been good enough. He shook his head and, unable to bear the solitude any longer, locked his office and took the steps two at a time up to CCU.

When he arrived, it was to see Lily lying on the bed, snuggled into her mother. The pain inside his heart twisted again. He was supposed to be part of this scene. *His* wife. *His* daughter. Nothing was going to keep him from them.

He strode over and when he caught Natasha's eye he half expected her to shake her head or brush him away, but instead she smiled brightly, beckoning him over.

'Hey, here's Daddy,' she said.

'I don't want to see him,' Lily mumbled.

Natasha frowned. 'Why ever not?'

'Because he didn't look after you like he promised me.'

'What? Of course he did. Daddy *did* look after me.'

Lily lifted her head and looked at her mother. Natasha read confusion in her daughter's eyes. 'But you got hurt.'

'That wasn't Daddy's fault.' She glanced up at Brenton. 'He did *everything* he could, Lil—*everything*—to stop Mummy from getting hurt, but…' Natasha tried to shrug her shoulders but winced in pain. Brenton edged closer and she felt warmed by his protectiveness. 'But sometimes, honey, things just happen. Right out of the blue they just happen, and there's nothing we can do to stop them. Daddy got hurt, too, remember?'

Lily nodded and snuggled back against her mother. 'Daddy didn't break his promise, Lily,' Natasha said firmly, resting her own head back on the pillows and closing her eyes. Her head was getting heavier by the minute due to the effort of keeping herself bright and cheerful for Lily. She couldn't do it any longer.

'Mum needs to rest now,' Aunt Jude said.

'I don't want to go,' Lily told them, snuggling even closer to Natasha. She accidentally knocked the drip and Natasha winced.

'Stay still, Lil,' Brenton said softly but firmly. 'Why don't you and Mummy have a little snooze together there and I'll see what I can do about getting Mum transferred to the ward?' He pulled up the side bed-rail as he spoke and placed a spare pillow between Natasha's right arm, which was around Lily, and the bars of the rail.

'Thanks,' she murmured, her eyes still closed.

Brenton smiled, glad he could give her just that little bit of extra comfort. 'My pleasure.' He headed to the nurses' station and returned a few minutes later to find Natasha and Lily sleeping peacefully.

'Having Lily here now is the best thing for her,' Jude murmured.

'Brian Newton, that's her orthopaedic surgeon, is going to pop in to review her but things are looking pretty good so I don't see why he wouldn't transfer her to the ward within the hour.'

'Any chance of a single room?'

'Absolutely. I've already checked.'

'That will help. How do you feel about Lily sleeping the night here?'

Brenton shook his head. 'I know she'd probably love it but Tash is going to have nurses coming in through the night, checking her drip, doing their obs. Also, Lily tends to talk in her sleep and I don't want her to wake Tash any more than she's already going to be woken. I'm also hoping that Brian will discharge her in a day or two. After all, it's not as though she's ignorant of the complications and she'll have the two of us watching her like hawks.'

'What about Lily missing school?'

'No. Tash wants Lily kept as much in her routine as possible. The weekend will be here soon enough and by then Tash will be five days post-op.' He looked at the two most important females in his life, sleeping all curled up together.

'How long do you think we should let them sleep?'

'For as long as they can,' he murmured, and pulled up a chair.

It was two hours later when Lily woke up. The nurses had done their obs with as little disturbance as possible and Brian had approved Natasha's transfer. Lily was still drowsy but coherent enough to realise she was leaving her mother.

'Draw me a picture at school,' Natasha said. 'Because I love your pictures and they make me so happy.' She kissed her daughter and allowed Jude to carry her away. Brenton blew her a kiss, still not sure where he stood with her. Was he back in her good books? He shook his head in bewilderment.

'Don't even try to understand the female mind,' Natasha said on a laugh and then started to cough. He came to her side quickly and held out a cup of water with a straw. 'It's far too complex,' she added once she'd had a couple of sips.

Brenton chuckled. 'Agreed. You look a lot better.'

'I feel it. How does my chart look?' She held out her hand.

'Uh-uh.' He waggled his finger at her. 'Patients aren't supposed to read their own charts.'

'Brenton!'

'Tash!' He lowered the bed-rail and leaned over to kiss her. 'Do you have any idea how utterly desirable you are?' he murmured close to her ear.

'If you'll excuse us for a moment, Dr Worthington,' one of the nurses said. Brenton pulled away slowly but not before planting a kiss on his wife's lips. He turned to see two nurses and two orderlies standing there, all of them grinning like Cheshire cats. 'It's time to transfer Dr Forest to the ward.'

'Then you can have all the privacy you need, mate,' an orderly said as he came forward.

Brenton chuckled. 'Lucky me.'

The nurses simply looked at him and shook their heads. 'How do you put up with him, Natasha?'

'With a great deal of patience.' Natasha smiled at him.

'Ha! You? Patience?' Brenton laughed and Natasha joined in. It was like old times. Like they'd always been. They'd been given a second chance!

Earlier that morning, both of them had been shot. There were still a lot of unresolved issues but his love for her was beginning to overflow. The primal protective instinct burst through him and once the transfer was complete and they were alone again, he wasted no time in bringing their lips together in a union both so desperately desired.

'Mmm,' she murmured dreamily when they finally came up for air.

'I love you, Tash.' He smoothed some hair from her face. 'I always have.'

Her eyes misted with tears and her lower lip began to wobble. 'I am so in love with you it hurts.'

He kissed her once more before tenderly wiping the tears from her eyes with a tissue. 'It's amazing when clarity of mind strikes.'

'I know what you mean. I saw you get shot today and realised, within the space of a heartbeat, that whatever happened between us all those years ago is irrelevant. It's what I feel for you *now* that is important.'

'But we still need to get to the bottom of things. I need to know, Tash. I need to face the fact that my mother lied to me. She took you and my daughter away from me and now I've missed so much.'

'We'll do a lot of catching up.'

'It's not only that. I trusted my mother, Tash, only to find everything was a lie.' He exhaled sharply and raked a hand through his hair. Natasha reached out for his hand and he took hers. 'The one thing I *do* know is that I love you, Natasha Jayne, and I love our daughter, too. I want us to be a family— a *real* family. Just like you've always dreamed of.'

'Oh, Brenton.' Natasha couldn't stop the tears. Her emotions were extremely raw but she didn't care. He settled his mouth over hers and she knew they were on their way to getting back that powerful and all-encompassing love they'd shared so many years ago.

The pattern for the next few days was set, with Brenton leaving Natasha after she'd fallen asleep each night and bringing Lily to the hospital to see her in the morning before school. Aunt Jude would come, too, and take Lily to school while Brenton went to work.

He would stop by between meetings and join her for a rushed lunch, and while she enjoyed this, there was nothing she wanted more than to just go home. She missed Lily desperately but knew she had to be grown-up about it and so focused hard on the physio and occupational therapy until the time came for Lily to be brought in for her afternoon visit.

On Thursday night Brenton had left earlier than usual and, unable to bear the solitude of her hospital room, Natasha reached for the phone.

'I was desperate to hear your voice,' she said. 'What are you doing?'

'Paperwork. What else?'

She sighed. 'I even miss paperwork.'

'I can bring some in for you to do. After all, you're not left-handed so you can still write.'

'At least my drip has been removed,' she acknowledged thankfully. 'What's the time? My watch is in my drawer and I can't be bothered reaching over to look at it.'

'Half past ten.'

'Lily got to sleep all right?'

'Yes.'

'I think we should put clocks in all the patients' rooms. It's quite annoying.'

'Then they would only sit there and stare at them and get depressed.'

'Hmm. You have a point.'

'Are you depressed?' he asked with concern.

'No, just impatient.'

He chuckled. 'That's my Tash. Impatient as always. How did your session go with the counsellor?'

'Not bad. How about yours?'

'Not bad.'

Natasha giggled. 'Brenton?' she said softly.

'Yes?'

'What are you wearing?' She heard his sharp intake of breath. 'Well? Aren't you going to tell me?'

'I wouldn't want to add to your impatience.'

'Aw, come on. Play by the rules.'

'I think you've had enough excitement for one day.'

'Excitement? You call physio and counselling sessions excitement?'

'Yes. The more you rest and relax like a good little girl, the sooner Brian will release you.'

'I tell you what, if he doesn't let me go home tomorrow, I'll be discharging myself.' Her words were forceful. 'I'm a doctor, for crying out loud. *You're* a doctor. Surely between the two of us we'll be able to pick up any warning signs.'

'Brian knows that, Tash.'

'It's boring in here.'

'Enjoy it while you can. You're usually rushed off your feet.'

'Yes, and I prefer that.'

'How are you going to handle the next six weeks of not working?'

'At least I'll be at home,' she grumbled despondently, and Brenton laughed. 'Quit stalling and answer the question.'

'What question?'

'What are you wearing?'

'And I've told you I'm not going to answer that question because I don't want you more frustrated than you already are.'

'I thought a frustrated woman was every man's dream because then they can solve all her problems and she'd be forever in their debt.'

'You might be right,' he said after careful consideration. 'Perhaps you should ask the sister for something to help you sleep.'

'Oh, ha, ha, very funny. Aren't you as frustrated as I am?'

'Naturally, but you'll be home soon enough.'

'Meaning?'

'Meaning you won't be locked up in hospital unable to do the things you…er…want to do.'

'Nice save.'

'I thought so.' He was quiet for a moment.

'What's wrong?'

'Nothing. Just Lily talking in her sleep.' Brenton saved his document and shut his laptop down before shifting in the bed.

'Where are you?' she asked, hearing him move.

'In bed—your bed. *Our* bed.'

Natasha gulped.

'Tash?'

'Yes?'

His voice had dropped an octave and was filled with a teasing pleasure. 'Are you blushing?'

'Yes.'

'Where?'

'Hey—I'm not going to answer that question until you answer mine.'

'I'm wearing boxer shorts.'

'I'm blushing all over.'

'Wish I was there.'

'No. Wish *I* was *there*.' She sighed with longing. 'I'm discharging myself tomorrow. That's the end of it.'

'No, honey,' he contradicted. 'It will only be the beginning.'

'Of what?'

'The next phase in our lives.'

Annie came by after getting off the night shift and enjoyed breakfast with Natasha. She was sitting on the bed, dressed in a white sleeveless shirt with buttons down the front and a pair of khaki shorts.

'I'm quite impressed with the food they give patients,' Annie remarked as she pinched a mouthful of Natasha's pancakes.

'It's not too bad.'

'Anxious to get out?'

'You said it.'

'I don't blame you. How's Lily been coping?'

Natasha shrugged. 'She's a child. They adapt more easily than us. Besides, she has Brenton and Aunt Jude at home.'

Annie nodded. 'Still, it can't have been easy for her, having you in hospital.'

'We didn't tell her exactly what happened to me. The best thing for children is to answer their questions when they ask them and not to go into too much detail. She's just too young to come to terms with the truth.'

'Definitely. So she's…coped fine…you know, with just having Monty and your aunt at home?'

'Yes.' Natasha took a sip of her tea and handed the plate with her pancakes to Annie. 'You may as well eat these. I'm not that hungry.'

'Isn't Monty bringing Lily in this morning?'

'He'd better.' Natasha looked at her watch. 'I've got another half-hour. I'm dressed, I've breakfasted…' She glanced at her tray and reached for her banana. 'Well, almost, and I've even packed my bag.'

Annie laughed. 'Ready to go, eh?'

'Absolutely. I'd like to get the nurses to page Brian Newton but I know he'll be around later this morning. It's just so…annoying.'

'How's your arm feeling?'

'Fine. Now, if only they'd let me out.'

'Well, they say that doctors make the worst patients.'

'Doctors *and* nurses, thank you very much, and I'm quite happy to prove that saying one hundred per cent correct.'

'Why are you so anxious to get home?'

'To get out from beneath the microscope.'

'I guess so, but isn't there another reason?'

'Just spit it out, Annie. Not the pancake.' Natasha laughed. 'You know what I mean.'

'Aren't you concerned that Monty and Jude are coping just a little too well with Lily without you?'

Natasha sighed. 'I don't like being left out and that's exactly how I feel. They've organised Lily so well, I guess she doesn't really need me after all.'

'Garbage.'

'Oh, I know she does but at the moment I feel, well…a little redundant. It's always been me and Lily. That's it. I moved to Geelong so we could be close to Jude because I know how important family is, having never really had one myself.'

'Were you abused?' The question was asked quietly.

'No. I went to boarding school when I was four years old and before that I had a nanny to raise me. I hardly saw my parents.'

'What about Aunt Jude?'

'She had no idea I existed until I was almost seventeen.'

'What happened then?'

'Aunt Jude came and got me.'

'Why didn't she come before?'

'She didn't know. She'd been travelling overseas and bumped into an old family friend. Aunt Jude and my dad are hardly close so she had no idea I even existed.' Natasha shook her head sadly. 'I'd lived most of my life at boarding school and for years I'd watched all the other girls get picked up by their parents for the holidays, but not me. Not once did I see my parents.'

'And so when Aunt Jude found out, she came and got you.'

'Yes.'

'Your parents didn't protest.'

'Nope. Nothing.'

'And you had no contact with them the whole time you were at the school?'

'None.' Natasha sniffed and reached for a tissue, amazed the emotions could still affect her. 'I did my final year of school in Melbourne and then went straight to med school.'

'Where you met Monty.'

'Well, yes. I'd seen him around on campus but he was two years ahead of me. We slowly became friends but it wasn't until my final year that we began to date. His mother was furious.'

'But he protected you from her?'

'As best he could…but she outsmarted us both.'

'No. She just…delayed things for a while.' Annie ate the last bite of pancake. 'Mmm, delicious.'

Natasha blew her nose and threw the tissue in the bin. 'I look at my life and can't believe it's turned out so…rocky. I mean, it's been just over four weeks since we left Wangaratta and my entire life has changed—again!'

'Do you love Brenton?'

Natasha smiled. 'Yes. I always have and I always will.'

'I'm sensing there's a *but* in there.'

'It all just seems too good to be true. That's what I thought all those years ago when we were first married. When I became pregnant with Lily, I still couldn't believe things were finally coming together for me.'

'And then Ma Worthington did her deed.'

Natasha laughed. 'Yes, she did.'

'But she didn't succeed.'

Natasha thought about that. 'I guess you're right.'

'Of course I'm right. You, Monty and Lily are all together again. One big happy family, with an aunt thrown in to boot.'

'And good friends.'

'Naturally.' Annie preened.

The door to her room burst open and Lily hurtled herself at Natasha's bed. 'Surprise, Mummy. I got up really early today so we could get here sooner, and now I can spend more time with you before Aunt Jude comes to take me to school. Isn't that a nice surprise? Were you surprised, Mum?'

'Very,' Natasha said, giving Lily a big squeezy hug. 'Ooh, I've missed you.'

'I missed you too, Mum.'

'Good morning, Tash.' Brenton placed a kiss on her lips. 'What have you and Annie been chatting about?'

'Never you mind,' Annie remarked. 'At any rate, now that I've stuffed myself full of Natasha's pancakes, I might go home and get some sleep.' She smothered a yawn as if to prove her point. 'I'll catch up with you tomorrow—at *home*.' Annie held up her crossed fingers before heading out.

'When can you come home, Mummy?'

'Well, I have to see the doctor first but hopefully today.'

'Today? Yippee.' Lily's happiness turned to panic and she placed a hand over her mouth and looked at Brenton. 'What about...?' she said in a whisper, but Brenton shook his head and put his finger against his mouth. Lily nodded knowingly.

'What are you two up to?' Natasha asked warily.

'Nothing,' Brenton replied with a smile.

'Yeah, nothing, Mum.'

'Hmm.' Lily climbed down off her bed and went over to whisper something to Brenton. He whispered something back. They were obviously planning a surprise for her and she didn't want to spoil it so she pretended to be eating the rest of her banana. Lily giggled excitedly and Natasha couldn't help but smile. Her girl was happy.

'I've just remembered,' Brenton said. 'I need to make a quick phone call.'

'Oh, well, here you go,' Natasha said, and pointed to the phone on her locker.

'That's all right. I'll use the one out on the ward.'

'Sorry. I didn't realise it was patient-related.'

He waved her concern away as he headed out. Lily climbed back on her bed.

'Mum?'

'Yes.'

'*I've* got a picture of daddy and me—'

'Daddy and I,' she corrected.

'Daddy and I by *my* bed now. He gave it to me this morning.'

'That's great. Is it in a picture frame?'

'Yes. A *gold* one, with love hearts around the edge.'

'Wow. That sounds really special.'

Brenton came back in and sat on the edge of her bed. 'Jude's been held up so she'll be in later this morning. That way, the two of you can have a good old chin-wag.'

'How will Lily get to school?'

'I can take her.'

'Goody,' Lily said brightly, clapping her hands. It wasn't long before it was time to go and Natasha was surprised that they were leaving a little earlier than usual.

'Just as well you came in a bit earlier,' she said as she kissed her daughter goodbye. 'Have a good day at school, honey.'

'I will. Love you, Mum.'

Natasha's heart swelled with maternal love and pride. 'Love you, too, princess.'

Brenton leaned over and kissed her. 'Get the nurses to page me when Brian arrives.'

'Will do, boss.'

'Miss me.' He kissed her again and reluctantly she watched them both leave.

'And then there was one,' she said mournfully.

The morning progressed and she *did* have a good time with Aunt Jude.

'It's nice to be able to sit and talk,' her aunt said while she knitted. 'Usually it's Lily or the dinner or something which needs attention—not that I'm complaining. Oh, no. I'm just saying it's nice to sit and chat with my niece.'

'Well, it's nice to have your company,' Natasha said. 'Especially as it seems that Brian has completely forgotten about me today.'

'What time is he usually here?'

'Anytime before midday, but it looks as though he's pushing it today!'

No sooner were the words out of her mouth than the man in question walked into the room, a nurse following behind.

'And about time, too,' Natasha muttered.

'I heard that.' Brian picked up her chart and read it.

'I think you'll find everything in order there,' she remarked.

'Yes, I do.'

'Oh, Brenton wanted to be paged when you arrived.'

'I've done that,' the nurse replied. 'He said he's on his way.'

'Thanks.'

Brian reviewed Natasha's arm and was pleased with her progress. When Brenton arrived, he handed down his verdict.

'I'm a little hesitant to let you go, but as you're showing no signs of compartment syndrome or any other complications, I guess I really have no reason for detaining you any longer.'

'Woo-hoo,' Natasha yelled.

'But at the first sign of even the remotest hiccup,' he warned both Brenton and her, 'I want to know about it.'

'Right.' Brenton promised. 'I'll make sure I keep a *very* close eye on her.' He rubbed his hand along the back of Natasha's neck and fiddled with her hair.

'I don't think I want to know about it.' Brian laughed. 'See you next week for a check-up,' he said to Natasha.

Brenton laughed when he saw Natasha's bag all packed and ready to go.

'Since six o'clock this morning,' she ventured, and he laughed again.

'Talk about impatient. What are we going to do with her, Jude?'

'That's none of my business,' her aunt replied with a cheeky grin as she packed up her knitting. 'I might leave you to take Natasha home. I want to stop by the shops and pick up a few things. Tonight should definitely be a celebratory dinner!'

'Here! Here!'

'I'll get Lily from school as well.'

'You're going to be out *that* long?' Natasha asked.

'I think you and Brenton need a bit of time to yourselves. Without the hospital, without Lily or me. Even if it's just for a few hours,' Jude replied.

'Thanks,' Brenton said, and leaned over to kiss Aunt Jude on the cheek.

'Charmer,' she replied, and blew a kiss to Natasha before leaving.

'Right. Let's get you discharged.' Brenton picked up her bag and off they went.

She noticed he was being extremely careful as he drove, making sure he didn't go around corners too fast, avoiding bumps and potholes in the road. When he parked the car in her driveway, he made her sit still while he came around and opened her door.

'Full service,' he said, and no sooner had she stepped out of the car than he swept her off her feet and carried her into the house, being careful of her left side. 'I know this isn't the first time I've carried you over the threshold,' he murmured in her ear, 'but this *is* a new beginning so it seemed appropriate.'

'Do you hear me complaining?' She was surprised when he continued up the passage. 'Where are we going?'

'Close your eyes.' After a moment's hesitation she obliged and he pushed her bedroom door open with his foot and carried her in. 'Keep them closed—I'm just putting you down on the bed.'

Natasha's heart began to race. Was he going to propose? The first time had been special when he'd wined and dined her at one of Melbourne's fanciest restaurants and then taken her for a moonlit drive in a limousine where he'd given her one single lily with an engagement ring fitted around the stem.

She breathed in appreciatively and caught the scent of not only him but something else in the room. It was sweet and with a mixed perfume. She heard him close the door and her hands began to perspire as she waited impatiently for him to say she could open her eyes. Was he going to be on bended knee or was he going to do something different?

'Open sesame,' he said at last and she felt her excitement escalate.

Slowly she opened her eyes and gasped. The room was decorated with beautiful fresh flowers of all colours and varieties. Across her mirror hung a sign.

CHAPTER TWELVE

WELCOME HOME, MUMMY had been coloured in with rainbow colours by Lily's loving hand. Although Natasha was mildly disappointed it wasn't a marriage proposal, she was still touched by the gesture.

'Is something wrong?' Brenton asked.

'Ah…no. No.' She smiled as she stood and walked over to the sign, touching it tenderly. 'Did she do it all by herself?'

'Absolutely. She's worked very hard on it. We went to the florist before school this morning and chose the flowers together.'

'So that's what you two were up to. Conspiracies at work.'

Brenton took her hand in his. 'Only good conspiracies.' He kissed her cheek. Then her forehead. Then her eyes. She breathed in deeply and leaned against him. Placing his arm possessively around her waist, he led her over to the bed.

'Let's get more comfortable, hmm?' He lay down on her right side, being careful of her left arm in the sling.

'Alone at last,' she murmured, and reached up to rub her fingers across the back of his neck. With a gentle pressure she urged his head down so their lips could meet. He pressed one feather-light kiss there, as though a tempting prelude to what might follow, and it certainly whetted her appetite.

He brushed his thumb across her lips and they parted. She breathed out and closed her eyes, relaxing back into the pillows. He moved his thumb to caress first her top lip and then the bottom, where she surprised him by flicking her tongue out and licking him. He sucked in a breath as a spark of desire rippled through him.

Desire burned deep within her and even though her left arm was completely out of action, she couldn't resist initiating a more intimate scenario with the man she loved. For the past few days she'd had to be content with quick kisses here and there and not once had she been able to initiate them. Even then, they'd generally had people in the room or the threat that anyone could walk in at any time. Frustration burned.

'Brenton,' she pleaded, and within seconds his mouth was covering hers in a hot and hungry kiss. The fire which had started to burn within her the instant she'd first laid eyes on him again began to rage out of control. He was sensitive as well as seductive and she was past the stage of refusing any of her emotions where he was concerned. She wanted him.

'Honey...' he murmured, his breathing uneven. Natasha didn't want to talk. She pulled his mouth back to hers and heard him groan with tormented pleasure. She didn't want logic, she didn't want common sense. She wanted to feel alive, to feel swamped by the emotions only *he* could evoke. Maybe that way it would help block out the other emotions which had been rearing their ugly heads since the shooting. Frustration...uncertainty...she didn't want them any more.

He took another breath and looked down into her face. She expected him to say something but instead he kissed her again. This time, although their breathing was still quite ragged, he changed the pace a little.

Softly...slowly...sensually.

He spread butterfly kisses across her forehead, around to her ear and down her neck. The valley between her breasts was next to fall victim to his ministrations but as the sling started to get in the way, it restricted him somewhat.

He worked his way back to her mouth and pressed one more hard, wet kiss to her lips. 'I want you so much, Tash,' he ground out harshly.

'I know.'

He rested his head next to hers while their breathing slowly returned to normal. Neither of them spoke and after about five more minutes Brenton realised she'd drifted off to sleep. He shouldn't have been surprised as her body had been through a lot lately.

He brushed her hair away from her face and settled down next to her. Just lying next to her brought back so many memories. It felt…right. They were each other's other halves and both had acknowledged as much when they'd first started dating.

She'd shifted slightly and had snuggled into him as best she could. Her breathing was long and deep—well, at least he'd helped her to relax. He took a deep breath and felt his own muscles relax, content in the knowledge that his wife was at his side.

Natasha couldn't believe how good she felt.

She sighed deeply as she opened her eyes, recalling a most wonderful dream. She stretched and was instantly made aware of her left arm in its sling. *Then* she became aware that she wasn't the only person in her bed.

She moved one leg and came into contact with another. Well, unless Lily had drastically grown, it couldn't possibly be her. As she breathed in, Brenton's scent surrounded her and she smiled. She was in bed with Brenton—well, lying on top of the covers fully clothed but, nevertheless, he was lying beside her.

He breathed in again and she realised he was snoring a little. That was probably what had woken her. She shifted a little so she could watch him, drink him in, but as she did so, he opened his eyes.

He sat up, instantly alert as most doctors were when dragged from sleep. 'Tash?'

'Shh.' She laughed lightly. 'I'm still here.'

He settled back beside her with relief. 'How's the arm? Everything all right?'

She snuggled back beside him. 'Everything's fine. Just fine.'

Brenton lifted his arm around her and she snuggled in more. He dropped a kiss on top of her head. 'This feels nice.'

'Mmm.' She closed her eyes again, her mind ticking over. 'Brenton?'

'Hmm?'

'Why don't you date? Either now or in the past?'

The question startled him and he thought of how best to answer it. 'Why do you ask?'

'Don't be coy,' she teased lightly. 'Deb told me you're a very sought-after guy. I mean, this hospital fundraiser everyone's talking about sounds like a big event.'

'It is. Why? Do you want to go?'

'Would *you* escort me?'

'Absolutely.'

'She just said that most of the nurses, at one time or another, have made a play for you. She mentioned that she'd asked you to the fundraiser and you'd politely declined.'

'She's not my type.'

'So you don't usually date?'

'No.'

'Why not?'

He drew in a deep breath and slowly exhaled. 'I guess it's hard to explain. When you left—'

'But I didn't.'

'I know, but let me tell it from my side of things. When I returned and found you gone I was very bitter. Angry, hurt. For the first few years I wasn't interested in the other sex and as far as trusting them went, well, forget it.'

'But you trust Annie.'

'She's different. One, I'm not romantically interested in Annie and, two, I've known her for too long so she doesn't count. After four or so years I gave in to my mother's constant nagging to settle down with a nice respectable woman.' He felt Natasha tense beneath his arm. 'She'd chosen a long list of socialites and none of them—*none* of them—made me feel the way you had. It was then I came to realise that my one true love—my soul-mate—had come and gone. There wasn't any point in dating.'

'Oh, Brenton.' Natasha moved carefully and leaned up to kiss him. Her heart was aching for the pain and mortification he must have carried around all those years. 'As I thought you'd died, I was at least able to grieve and slowly make a new start on my life.' She kissed him again. 'But it wasn't meant to be. *Here! This* is where I'm meant to be. I've thought a lot in the last few days about what's happened. I was *shot*, Brenton. A few more centimetres over and the bullet would have hit my heart.'

'Don't!' The word was wrenched from him and he held her close.

'I have to. I have to face this. I've been through therapy before, Brenton, through the grieving process, and I've learnt the hard way that I have to face my emotions. I can't lock them away and ignore them because they only fester. If I don't search for some justification for the emotions I'm feeling then I'm going to end up in an even bigger mess—and so are you.' She shook her head. 'I'm not going to let that happen to us. We're both people who prefer plain speaking as opposed to riddles and meaningless psycho-babble.

'I *know* you and you *know* me—better than anyone. We've found each other again. Can you believe that? After all this time, after everything that has happened to us, we've found each other. We belong together.'

'You're right, Tash.' He sat up and pulled her gently to face him. She saw concern in his eyes and started to feel a little uneasy.

'Brenton? What's wrong?'

'There's something I need to tell you.' Taking both her hands in his, he gave them a reassuring squeeze. 'I contacted a solicitor about the divorce decree.'

'And?'

'And the divorce was never filed.'

'What? Why not?'

'It was drawn up by a disbarred solicitor. I didn't know that at the time and believed the papers had come from your solicitor.'

Natasha nodded. 'Your mother wanted you to believe you were divorced so if you chose to remarry in the future, you would be able to.'

'More than likely.'

'But then…' Natasha frowned as she thought it through. 'If you had remarried then you would have committed bigamy.'

'Yes.' Brenton watched her closely as more of the pennies started to drop. She gasped, her eyes wide with shock.

'This means…we're…still…' She tried to control her breathing as she continued to work it out. 'And *I* remarried so…*I've*…already committed…' She trailed off and covered her mouth with her hand. 'Oh, Brenton!' She shook her head, trying to deny it. 'I could go to gaol!'

'It's all right. It's all right,' he soothed, and took her in his arms, cradling her tenderly, frustrated that he couldn't hold her properly. 'That's why I needed the death certificate. I gave it to Pierce and he contacted a friend of his who specialises in federal law. His friend has been away and was due back today so hopefully we'll have an answer pretty soon.'

Natasha couldn't believe it. She just couldn't believe it. Just when she thought her life was coming up roses, *this* had to happen! Her disbelief started to bubble into anger and she pushed out of his embrace. 'Why are you just telling me this now? Why didn't you tell me about this sooner?'

'Because I wanted to protect you. I was going to tell you the morning of the shooting. Remember I said we needed to talk? I was going to tell you everything that night.' He raked a hand through his hair. 'You've been through so much, Tash. Not only with what's happened to us but with the shooting. I'm your husband. I *need* to protect you and I haven't done a very good job of it lately.' He reached out a hand to her but she moved away.

'Don't touch me.'

'Why are you mad with *me?*'

'Why didn't you fight harder? Why didn't you protect me, Brenton? Why didn't you hunt me down and find out the truth for yourself?'

'I tried,' he insisted vehemently. 'I did everything I could to try and track you but you'd disappeared without a trace. I was also hurt and confused. Come on, Tash. I was twenty-

five years old. I was humiliated and depressed. I pushed myself to the nth degree. After I qualified, I worked in a war
zone for two years, hoping I'd get shot.'

Natasha gasped.

Brenton raked a hand through his hair. 'You'd killed me
on the inside, Tash,' he said more softly. 'You'd taken my
heart and ripped it to shreds. Life just wasn't the same any
more.' He reached for her again and this time she didn't pull
away. He held her hand protectively in both of his. 'Ironically
enough, my mother was the only woman I trusted. She was
dead set against me going overseas to work but I needed to
get out of the country. When I returned she looked older and
more frail and I felt guilty for the worry I'd caused her. I
listened to her advice, although I didn't necessarily act on it.
She may have told me to start dating again, organising my
life for me, but you know the old saying, "You can lead a
horse to water—"'

'"But you can't make him drink,"' Natasha finished.

'You're the only woman I want. No.' He shook his head.
'You're the only woman I *need*.' He laughed humourlessly.
'In the past few weeks, I've learnt so much—changed so
much.'

'We both have.'

'Our lives have changed, Tash…for the better. You've
made me realise that it's *you* who I trust. You've *never* lied
to me and slowly the emotional scarring around my heart is
beginning to heal. Thanks to you.'

He leaned forward and kissed her.

It was a kiss of promise.

A kiss of hope.

A kiss of love.

His mobile phone rang and he groaned, pulling away reluctantly. He snapped it off his belt. 'Dr Worthington.' He
waited. 'What's the news, Pierce?' He looked expectantly at
Natasha and whispered, 'My solicitor.' Brenton listened and
raised his eyebrows. 'So this is all sorted out now?'

Natasha could feel the dread building within her. 'What?' she asked quietly, but Brenton only nodded.

'Thanks, mate. I owe you one.' He disconnected the call.

'Well?'

'Everything's all right.'

'What? What does that mean? Did I commit bigamy?'

'Yes, but as the death certificate is forged, you did it unknowingly. Therefore you are not classified as the guilty party and no charges will be brought against you.'

Relief flooded her and she sagged back onto the bed.

'He also said the death certificate and the divorce decree were done by the same people.'

She shook her head. 'Was my signature on the divorce forms?'

'Yes. You know when you said you signed forms in the hospital but you couldn't remember what they were?'

'Of course.' She closed her eyes, unable to believe she'd been so stupid. 'Oh, Brenton,' she whispered, tears forming beneath her eyelids. 'If only—'

'Don't go there, Tash. It's over.' He kissed her softly. 'Look at me.' He waited for her to open her eyes. 'It's over, honey. We'll have each other for ever.' He wiped away her tears. 'I love you, Tash.'

She breathed a deep, cleansing breath and nodded, turning her head so she could gaze into his deep, blue eyes. 'I love you, too, B.J.'

He smiled and kissed her possessively. The emotions he stirred within her rocked her to the core. He was alive—they both were, and they had a future together. His mouth left hers but only to nibble and kiss his way down her neck towards her ear. 'Tash?' He whispered her name like a cherished caress.

'Hmm?' She closed her eyes.

'What are you wearing?'

A slow smile spread across her lips as his hand started to slide its way up her body. 'A sling.'

He stopped, lifted his head and looked down at her arm

'Oh, yeah.' His look of disappointment made her laugh and he collapsed on the bed next to her.

'Mummy?' Lily's high-pitched call came through the house. 'Mummy?'

Brenton sat up and started to move but Natasha stopped him. 'Don't go.'

Loud footsteps echoed as they heard Lily run up the hallway. 'In here,' Natasha called, and sat up.

'You're home!' Lily squealed, as she launched herself onto Natasha's bed.

'Careful,' both parents said in unison. Lily flung her arms around Natasha's neck and pressed kisses all over her face.

'My mummy's home. Do you like my poster?'

'I *love* it, honey, and I'm going to keep it for ever.' Natasha kissed Lily's head. 'The flowers are beautiful, too. Both you and Daddy did an excellent job decorating my room. It was a lovely surprise, Lil. Thank you.'

'It was my idea—oh, and guess what?' She jumped off the bed and disappeared down the hallway again. Brenton and Natasha looked at each other in amusement as Lily came pounding back, her schoolbag in tow, a white form in her hand. 'This is from the guitar teacher. She said that you had to sign it so I can play guitar. Can I, Mum? Can I? *Please?*'

Natasha smiled at her daughter. She'd spoken to Lily's teacher the previous week to find out more about it but hadn't given it another thought. She looked at Brenton, who seemed to have the same pleading look on his face. It was then she realised that allowing Lily to learn guitar would give both Brenton and Lily something unique and special in common. It would help them bond and it would be something for just the two of them.

Tears welled in her eyes as she realised that, no matter what, they would all be together for ever. One big happy family.

Finally she nodded. 'All right.'

'Yippee!' She flung her arms around Natasha again and bounced up and down on the bed. Natasha was just about to ask her to stop when Lily hurtled herself at Brenton. 'I can use your guitar, Daddy, and you can help me.'

'You bet.' Brenton kissed his daughter.

'You've got to practise at least twice a week.'

'I will.'

'I'll make sure of it,' Brenton remarked, and shifted so he could embrace both his girls. 'I'm the happiest man in the world.'

EPILOGUE

Two weeks later the hospital was abuzz with the excitement of the fundraiser.

Natasha stood in front of the mirror, trying to put her new ruby earrings in but they just weren't co-operating.

'Need some help, Dr Worthington?' Brenton said as he walked into their bedroom.

'It's so frustrating and so is this sling. When can it come off, Brenton?'

'Hey, don't look at me. I'm your husband, not your doctor.' He kissed her before taking the earrings from her and patiently hooking them through the holes in her earlobes. 'There. All done.' He took a step back from her, his gaze caressing her from top to toe. 'You look…stunning.'

'I'm wearing a sling, Brenton.'

He smiled. 'You still look stunning. Are you sure we have to go?' He raised his eyebrows suggestively.

'Yes.' She laughed and smoothed her hand down the white crêpe fabric of her strapless dress. Her left ring finger was adorned with the engagement and wedding ring that Brenton had given her all those years ago. Around her neck was a ruby and diamond necklace which matched her earrings. Both had been gifts from Brenton, which he had requested she wear this evening. He'd also insisted that her hair be loose. He took a lock in his hand and let his fingers slide through it.

'Glorious.' He stepped forward and kissed her, his mouth possessive on hers.

'Don't smudge my make-up.'

'I wouldn't dream of it.' He crooked his arm to her. 'Ready?'

'Ready.'

Lily was a bundle of excitement as they said goodnight, which Natasha thought was rather strange. Usually if she had to go out to functions like this, Lily was all pouty and sulky because she wanted to go as well. Then again, notwithstanding the guitar lessons, Lily had been extremely happy during the past weeks. In fact, they'd all been happy.

Natasha settled back into the comfortable leather passenger seat of Brenton's Jaguar as he drove them to the function centre.

'You know, Tash, I've been thinking,' he said after a pause.

'Really? Did it hurt?'

He smiled and took her hand in his, holding it firmly against his thigh. 'How would you feel about renewing our wedding vows?'

Natasha was surprised. 'Uh…sure. If you want to.'

'I do, but do *you* want to?'

She thought about it for a moment. 'Yes. It would be good for Lily, too.'

'That's what I thought.' He brought her hand to his lips and kissed it.

When they arrived at the function centre, they had to park down the street due to the impressive turnout. 'I really don't like formal things like this,' he said, fiddling with his bow-tie.

'Leave it alone,' Natasha reprimanded, and tapped his hand down. 'You look incredible in a tux so just relax and enjoy the evening.'

'Good advice,' he murmured as they entered the throng.

Many people welcomed them, the hospital now accepting the fact that their most eligible bachelor was definitely off the market. The evening progressed and once dinner and dessert, as well as the official announcements, had been attended to, the band started playing.

Brenton leaned over and whispered in her ear, 'Care to dance, my wife?'

She turned and smiled at him. 'I'd love to, my husband.' He held her chair before leading her onto the dance floor. The music turned to a slow number and he gathered her carefully into his embrace.

'Maybe we should gang up on Brian tonight because this sling is beginning to frustrate me as well,' he growled softly into her ear.

'Sounds like a plan to me.' She laughed.

The MC for the evening broke into the music, asking the band to stop playing as he had an important announcement to make. Natasha stopped dancing and started heading back to her seat, but Brenton stopped her, holding her firmly by his side.

'We have a very special event happening tonight, ladies and gentlemen, and I'm *not* talking about the fundraiser. Would those involved please come forward?'

Again Natasha tried to go back to her seat but Brenton held her to him. 'Just stay here for a second, Tash,' he said.

She looked around and felt her jaw drop open as she saw Aunt Jude and Lily walking towards them. Behind them were some of her good friends from Wangaratta, including Matthew and Kelly Bentley.

Natasha was stunned.

When she turned back to look at Brenton, he merely smiled and got down on bended knee, holding her right hand in his. Everyone started clapping and a few people wolf-whistled. The MC asked everyone to quieten down and in a loud, clear voice, Brenton spoke.

'You once married me for better or worse. We've come through some very tough years but our love has never died.' He motioned for Lily to come to his side and the little girl, dressed in a beautiful white dress with dainty ballet slippers on her feet, came running to his side, her curls bouncing around her head. She stood beside her father who enveloped her with his free arm.

'I love you, Tash. I always have and I always will. I love our daughter and together the three of us make a family. Marry me again, Tash. Marry me tonight.'

Lily put her arms around his neck and he stood, lifting her with him.

'Well, Mummy?' Lily demanded impatiently, and people laughed.

'How can my answer be anything other than…yes!' She leaned into Brenton. 'I love you, too, and you, my darling girl.' She kissed Lily on the nose.

A woman standing beside them cleared her throat and Natasha turned to look at her. 'Good evening, dear,' the woman said. 'I'm the marriage celebrant and I'd be honoured if you'd allow me to guide you and your husband in renewing your vows.'

Tears gathered in Natasha's eyes. Tears of sheer joy.

She looked at Aunt Jude and motioned her over. She beckoned Matt and Kelly to come closer, too. These people were her family, regardless of whether or not they shared the same blood. True family relationships began with the heart and tonight she would accept this most precious gift from the people who meant the world to her.

'Ready?' the celebrant asked.

Natasha gazed up at Brenton and then at Lily. She nodded. 'Ready.'

They renewed their vows in front of everyone present and Natasha had never felt more content in her life.

'Do you have the ring?' the celebrant asked, and Brenton turned to Lily. She squirmed in Brenton's arms and he ended up having to put her on the ground. She dug her little fingers into the tiny pocket hidden in the seam of the dress, her tongue between her teeth as she concentrated.

He bent to help her but she brushed him away. 'I can do it, Daddy.'

People laughed and Natasha smiled at her daughter's independence. It would serve her well.

Finally, Lily produced the ring and there was a round of applause. Brenton carefully took the fingers of her left hand in his and slid a ruby and diamond ring on so it was nestled in front of her other two rings.

'An eternity ring,' he stated. 'Because I promise to love you for eternity.'

'You may now kiss your wife,' the celebrant announced, and he did—long and thoroughly. People clapped, whistled and generally made a noise, but Natasha heard none of it.

'Mummy?' Lily asked, when Brenton finally released his wife from their embrace. Lily tugged at her mother's dress and Brenton picked her up again. 'Mummy?'

'Yes.'

'Are you happy?'

'Very.'

'Very, very happy?'

'Yes.'

'Good. Well, can I do gymnastic lessons? Because Gabrielle, my friend at school, well, she does gymnastic lessons and she showed me how she does twirls and stands on her hands and rolls and all sorts of things, and it looks really easy and I really think I could do it.'

Natasha laughed and looked at Brenton.

'We'll see!' they said in unison.

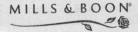

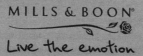

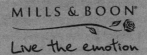

MILLS & BOON®

Live the emotion

Medical Romance™

DR SOTIRIS'S WOMAN by *Margaret Barker*

Dr Francesca Metcalfe is the most gorgeous woman Dr Sotiris Popadopoulos has ever seen, and while they are working together on Ceres Island he hopes they will get to know each other better. But it seems that Francesca has chosen her career over having a family, and Sotiris has his young son who is need of a mother…

HER SPECIAL CHILD by *Kate Hardy*

One look at locum GP Tina Lawson and Dr Alex Bowen is smitten – surely she must feel the same? She certainly does – but she can't risk getting involved with Alex. Her son Josh needs all her love and attention.   But Alex is determined to prove passion will last – and two is better than one when it comes to caring for such a special little boy.

EMERGENCY AT VALLEY HOSPITAL
by *Joanna Neil*

Mistaking consultant Jake Balfour for a patient is bad enough – and if only he weren't so attractive… When Carys's sister is injured Jake's support is unexpected – but ever since her troubled childhood Carys has sworn off men. Could Jake be the man to change her mind?

On sale 4th July 2003

Available at most branches of WH Smith, Tesco, Martins, Borders, Eason, Sainsbury's and all good paperback bookshops.

0603/03b

FREE

4 BOOKS
AND A SURPRISE GIFT!

We would like to take this opportunity to thank you for reading this Mills & Boon® book by offering you the chance to take FOUR more specially selected titles from the Medical Romance™ series absolutely FREE! We're also making this offer to introduce you to the benefits of the Reader Service™ —

- ★ FREE home delivery
- ★ FREE monthly Newsletter
- ★ FREE gifts and competitions
- ★ Exclusive Reader Service discount
- ★ Books available before they're in the shops

Accepting these FREE books and gift places you under no obligation to buy; you may cancel at any time, even after receiving your free shipment. Simply complete your details below and return the entire page to the address below. *You don't even need a stamp!*

YES! Please send me 4 free Medical Romance books and a surprise gift. I understand that unless you hear from me, I will receive 6 superb new titles every month for just £2.60 each, postage and packing free. I am under no obligation to purchase any books and may cancel my subscription at any time. The free books and gift will be mine to keep in any case.

M3ZED

Ms/Mrs/Miss/Mr ....Initials ....
BLOCK CAPITALS PLEASE

Surname ....

Address ....

....

....Postcode ....

Send this whole page to:
UK: FREEPOST CN81, Croydon, CR9 3WZ
EIRE: PO Box 4546, Kilcock, County Kildare (stamp required)

Offer valid in UK and Eire only and not available to current Reader Service subscribers to this series. We reserve the right to refuse an application and applicants must be aged 18 years or over. Only one application per household. Terms and prices subject to change without notice. Offer expires 30th September 2003. As a result of this application, you may receive offers from Harlequin Mills & Boon and other carefully selected companies. If you would prefer not to share in this opportunity please write to The Data Manager at the address above.

Mills & Boon® is a registered trademark owned by Harlequin Mills & Boon Limited.
Medical Romance™ is being used as a trademark.